The Monster of Montvale Hall

Saints & Sinners Book 1

NADINE MILLARD

*To Nelly for the love, support,
and unbreakable bond.*

Prologue

"STOP RUNNING SO fast. I can't keep up."

Robert Forsythe ignored the cries of his little sister, choosing instead to increase his pace as he ran toward the river.

"Ignore her," he yelled to his fellow escapees, his three best friends from Eton. Each of them the son and heir of a powerful Peer. Each of them determined to enjoy this precious time outside where they didn't have to be students, didn't have to be heirs to powerful titles, and didn't have to learn anything of their future responsibilities.

While staying at Robert's home for the Easter break from school, they all wanted to just be children. Just for a little while. Even though they were on the unsteady cusp of manhood.

And Robert didn't want Gina ruining it for them, slowing them down. It was irritating in the extreme to have his stubborn little sister following them around. James's brother, Thomas, was only a year or two older than Gina and he hadn't come after them. He'd stayed behind, like he'd been told to do. Gina would never do as she was told!

It had been storming for days, wind and rain lashing against the window panes of Montvale Hall, making it impossible for the boys to get outside.

The young marquess had never been one for sitting still and had been driven mad being cooped up inside. Though nobody could ever say that the Hall, the seat of his father, The Duke of Montvale, was small enough to feel cooped up in.

Still, there was only so much sport to be had in the cavernous halls filled with irreplaceable family heirlooms.

Even today, the winds were still a force to be reckoned with. But since it was dry, the duchess had agreed to let the boys out for a little while.

"Stay away from the river," she had warned, her tone brooking no argument.

The river current was, according to Mama, dangerously strong after inclement weather and so, of course, that was the first place a group of fourteen-year-old boys would head.

Growing up rarely hearing the word "no" lent them all a false sense of confidence in their own sensibilities.

"Bobby, *please.*"

Robert swung back to face his sister, his grey eyes flashing with the frustration that only an older brother could feel.

"Gina, get back to the house," he yelled over the

howling of the wind.

The sky had darkened ominously even as they'd tramped across the grounds of the estate.

"Robert, perhaps we should go back."

Robert turned to face his closest friend, the future Marquess of Avondale, with a grimace.

"Don't be silly, James. We've been stuck indoors for days."

"The weather is turning quite badly, and Gina shouldn't be out in this."

Robert's temper flared. No, Gina shouldn't be out in this. But Gina wasn't *supposed* to be out in this.

"The others are gone ahead," Robert said mutinously, pointing to where his two other close friends, Simon and Nicholas, could be seen headed toward the brook.

James looked hesitantly from Gina to their friends.

"You go ahead," he said finally. "I'll walk Gina back to the Hall and come back to you."

Robert felt an immediate swell of anger. It was so typical of James, the golden boy. Always doing what he should. Always doing what was right.

Robert hated that James made him feel lacking or not good enough.

"No, she's my baby sister," he bit out, resentful of the duty that fell to him.

"I'm not a baby," Gina shouted mutinously, and Robert had to smile in spite of himself.

In truth, even though he felt like he could happily ring her neck at times, he doted on Gina and had his mood not been so foul from being stuck inside for days at a time, he likely would have indulged her from the start.

"Gina, if I let you come, you must stay by my side. Do you understand?"

His sister's light grey eyes, so like his own, lit up at once, and he allowed himself a brief smile.

"I really don't think that's a good idea," James insisted.

Robert's stomach flip-flopped with uneasiness. Mama would have his head if she found out he'd allowed Gina to accompany them to the river—they weren't supposed to be headed there, either.

Nonetheless, he had always looked after her, and he would do so now.

"Come, James, by the time we get her back to the Hall the others will be wanting to return. We can watch her well enough."

James hesitated again, annoying Robert once more.

In truth, he and James were the best of friends with only months between them in age. But James was just so *good* all the time. Mama often joked that Robert was the anti-James, though Robert wasn't sure how much she was actually joking.

Robert's mother was James's godmother. And when James's mother had died in childbirth whilst the boys were toddlers, the Duchess of Montvale had become a sort of surrogate aunt to James, and he spent more time at Montvale than at his own future seat, Avondale Abbey.

Fathers, the boys had been informed, were not cut out to look after children.

Finally, after what seemed an age, James relented.

"Fine, come along then Gina." James smiled indulgently at his little honorary cousin. "If you get soaked to the bone or catch a chill, we shall just blame Robert."

Gina clapped her hands excitedly and then dashed off after Simon and Nicholas.

"She will be a handful when she's older," Robert said, not entirely sure what that meant, but he'd heard his father say so enough times to think it must be true.

"Yes, and she will also be your problem," James said with a laugh.

The two boys raced off after Gina, pushing, shoving, and jostling each other as they went.

They reached the bridge over the river just as the first, fat raindrops began to fall.

"Blast it all," Robert said.

"We must go back," Simon called from where he sat on the bridge with Nicholas, their legs dangling carelessly over the river.

The water was rushing furiously under the bridge, as high as Robert had ever seen it, and that feeling of uneasiness grew tenfold.

All of a sudden, it really didn't feel like a good idea to have Gina here.

"Yes," he agreed swiftly. "We must. Come, Gina."

Robert darted his glance around but couldn't see his sister.

The uneasiness grew instantly to foreboding.

"Gina!" he called, and James, Nicholas, and Simon began looking around, too.

"Gina, where are you?" he called.

"I'm here, you goose."

Robert whipped around, and an immediate fear clawed at him.

Gina was sitting atop a low branch of one of the many trees that bordered the river.

Robert had often stood on the same branch and jumped into the cool water of the river on hot summer days.

But it was far too dangerous for seven-year-old Gina to be on it, especially alone. And especially in the middle of a storm.

"Gina, come down here at once," he shouted, dashing over to the tree. "It isn't safe."

His impertinent little sister merely rolled her eyes.

"You always do it," she argued stubbornly.

"I am older," Robert said. "And the river is dangerous today."

"You sound just like Mama," Gina laughed.

"If you don't come down this instant, I will come

up there and fetch you myself," Robert warned.

"Oh, Bobby—" How could a little girl sound so long-suffering? "You are so—"

It was a second, a split second. But long enough for Robert to know that something was terribly, terribly wrong.

There was a distinctive snap, and Gina's eyes widened with fear.

In the next moment, Robert watched the branch give, and though it took mere seconds, it felt like a lifetime.

There was only a short, terrified scream before the branch and his little sister crashed into the river below.

"Gina!"

One of the boys roared. It could have been him. It could have been James.

And Robert, God help him, hesitated.

Fear had him frozen in shock.

Only James brushing past brought him out of it.

His eyes couldn't look away. The branch bobbed to the surface and then seconds later, his sister's blonde curls appeared.

Finally, his brain kicked into action and he darted forward.

"What do we do?" Nicholas called in panic.

He heard James shout something, but he didn't pay any attention.

Without conscious thought, Robert ran to the bank

and dove into the river.

Somewhere outside his bubble of terror, he knew the others were shouting his name.

The moment he hit the icy, tumultuous water, all the air left his body with the shock, and immediately the current gripped him.

It was so strong. Too strong.

Frantically, he looked around, even as the current tried to drag him under, to pull him away.

All he needed was just a glimpse of her.

There!

A flash of blonde against the greys and blacks surrounding him caught his eye.

Using all of his strength, Robert swam toward that flash of colour.

He prayed to God with all his might that he get there in time.

As though the Lord Himself had answered Robert's prayers, when he reached out, he managed to grab a handful of cotton from Gina's dress.

"I've got you," he shouted.

Gina was caught, her dress tangled in some reeds on the riverbed.

Robert pulled her tiny body against his chest, terrified of the shivers wracking her body, oblivious to his own.

The rain lashed in earnest now, making it almost impossible to see, and the wind howled as though bemoaning the fate of the children by the riverside.

Gina was turning blue and gasping for breath.

"It's alright, Gina. I have you."

Robert repeated the litany over and over again even as he inwardly panicked.

How would he get her out of the water? How would he make sure she survived this waking nightmare?

"Robert!"

Robert looked up and saw James and Nicholas at the banks, mere feet above him.

Thank God.

Both boys lay down, their hands stretching toward Robert and Gina.

"Simon is gone for help," James shouted.

"We need to get her out of the water," Robert called back, not caring about anything else.

The others nodded their understanding.

Robert, with Herculean effort, tried to lift Gina toward James, but his little sister gripped desperately to his shoulders, her eyes wide with panic.

"Gina, you must let go," Robert shouted above the wind, terror making his voice harsh.

"I-I c-can't!" She shivered, and Robert felt his eyes fill with tears.

This was beyond any horror he could ever imagine.

"You must," he insisted. "We need to get out of the water."

Gina stared at him for a moment, tears or rainwater streaming down her little face.

Finally, eons later, she nodded her head.

"Good girl," Robert said with relief as he felt her grip loosen.

But his fleeting relief was short-lived.

The second Gina's hands left his person, the unforgiving current snatched her body, and she shot away from him, as though pulled by an invisible whipcord.

"No!" Robert screamed, his hand darting out after her.

He managed to grip her fingertips, though both his and hers were icy with cold, and the merciless water rushed over their clasped hands, desperately trying to drag them apart.

"Pull me up," he yelled desperately.

He felt two pairs of hands on his jacket, as his cousin and his friend began the laborious task of pulling his drenched body from the water.

"Gina," he called, "hold on."

But he saw it then—the look that would haunt him for the rest of his miserable life. The look that no innocent child's eyes should hold. The look of someone who knew her life was about to end.

"Please," he sobbed. He couldn't even try to grab her tighter, could gain no more purchase on the bank or with her hand.

"Please, Gina. Hold on."

Though it should have been impossible with the cacophony of angry sounds the storm and river produced, Robert heard her whisper as clear as a bell. As clear as if she said it inside his very soul.

"Bobby, I'm scared."

Robert's heart clenched painfully. When Gina had been younger, she hadn't been able to pronounce the letter R properly and had taken to calling him Bobby. The name had stuck and became Gina's special name for him. She was the only one who used it and hearing it now from her blue, trembling lips was more painful than he could handle.

He couldn't speak. Could offer no word of comfort.

He began to pull against the hands dragging him to safety.

If Gina was going to let go, he would follow her. He wasn't going to watch her float away.

"Let go of me, James. She's slipping."

Perhaps they didn't hear. Perhaps they thought it better to save him, even though it was the worst thing they could do.

But they held on.

And Gina's grip loosened.

Within seconds, it was over.

Her tiny fingers slipped inevitably from his grasp.

Robert heard his own screams as though they came from someone else.

It was all so sudden.

One minute her tiny body floated, like a rag doll.

The next, it was gone, the river finally victorious in claiming a life.

Robert, on the bank now, fought with all his might to get away from the hands holding him back.

"Robert, she's gone. She's gone."

James' tearful voice sobbed in his ear as he clung furiously to his friend. But Robert wouldn't believe it. He couldn't.

Robert felt bile rise in his throat, and he turned toward the sodden ground, casting up his accounts.

Seconds or hours later, voices sounded all around him. Shouts of despair, screams of agony, yells of concern.

Someone threw a blanket around his shoulders and lifted him bodily into a cart.

Please, please, please don't let it be real. Please. Don't let it be real.

As the chills battered his body, Robert's head swam, and he prayed for the darkness that threatened on the edge of his consciousness. Welcomed it like an old friend.

He wanted it to come. And he wanted to remain in it forever.

Chapter One

ROBERT AWOKE WITH a start, jerking up in his bed, his skin glistening with sweat.

It took longer than usual for the blind panic to subside.

His heart pounded with remembered fear, and his mind replayed the expression on her face, the fear in her eyes, her fingers slipping through his over, and over, and over.

It had always been thus when the anniversary of Gina's death was approaching.

A death that he was responsible for.

That day had affected them all, he knew.

His father had taken to alcohol and become steadily more reliant on it as the years went on.

Robert had no doubt that was what had killed his sire eight years ago. That was the reason he was now the Duke of Montvale.

His mother was still alive, though existing might be a better description.

Her spirit had died the day Gina was swept away from them all, and she was nothing more than a shell of the person she'd once been.

Even his friends had been affected by Gina's death.

But then, Robert supposed, nobody could escape such a thing unscathed. Tragedies have a way of imprinting on one's soul. Something shifts inside you when you've lived through something awful. You go on with your life, but you're a different person than the one you once were.

And while James, Simon, and Nicholas had managed to recover from the drowning tolerably well, Robert couldn't go a day without the guilt and grief of that day gnawing at him.

Gina had been his sister, of course. But more than that—he'd been to blame.

Nobody had ever said so, but they didn't have to. He could see the indictment in the bottom of his father's empty brandy bottles, and in the sad vagueness of his mother's eyes, eyes that never quite focused on a person anymore.

Over the years, Robert had withdrawn more and more from his friends and loved ones.

He was fortunate, he supposed, in that Montvale Hall was situated in the stark, rugged isolation of Northumberland. Though the farmlands were hugely profitable and the village that owed its success to the estate was thriving, the Hall itself was set apart from everyone and everything, and Robert liked it that way.

He and his mother could stay here, haunted by the

things he didn't do to save Gina. Safe from pity and gossip.

Neither of them had ever been inclined to live at one of the other many houses he owned.

He kept only a skeletal staff. After all, there was only himself and his mother to take care of.

Montvale Hall had once hosted house parties, balls, and dinners to rival London in the height of the Season.

But no more.

It was now a haven for solitude and isolation. Dark, unforgiving. Like its master.

Robert wasn't deaf to the things that were said about him.

Servants talked. And townsfolk talked to servants.

He knew, for example, that people greatly pitied his mother for the hard life she had endured.

He knew also they had dubbed him the Monster of Montvale Hall.

A derisive grin, fleeting and unwelcome, crossed his face.

They weren't wrong, either. He was a monster of the worst kind. A monster responsible for the death of a child.

Robert scrubbed a hand over his face then jumped from the bed, filled with a restless agitation.

He knew that sleep would elude him for the remainder of the night. After a bad nightmare, sleep never again came. Or Robert never let it, in any case. Too terrified of what lurked behind his closed lids.

No, he would get no more rest this night.

Although, he acknowledged, as his storm-grey eyes took in the carriage clock on the mantle, it was already morning.

The household was still abed at this time, but in mere hours they would be up and bustling about, preparing a breakfast that would go largely untouched.

He moved to the window, pulling back the drapes to peer at the familiar landscape outside, gaining a sort of peace in the familiar view.

His rooms were at the back of the Hall. He'd relocated the master chamber as soon as he'd become the duke.

As far away from the view of the river as he could manage.

Now, all he saw were the acres and acres of his land. On a clear day, he'd be able to spy the rugged coastline in the distance.

How many times had he thought of running out there, toward the inevitable drop of the cliffs? Towards freedom from his torment?

Alas, he didn't have it in him. Whether that made him brave or cowardly, he had no idea. Perhaps just stupid.

Robert pressed the heel of his hand against his forehead. Usually after a nightmare, his head began to pound.

He'd be tempted to drown himself in whiskey, but he actually needed his wits about him today.

For today, James would arrive, seeking a favour.

His note had been mysterious. James had written to say he was coming to stay, and he was bringing along something that needed looking after. Shamelessly begging favours.

Robert had felt a twinge of curiosity.

As the influential Marquess of Avondale, James's power was only a step below Robert's own. And he was rich as Croesus, having inherited all of his family's old money and then expanding on it with business interests here and in the Americas.

What on earth could he need from Robert?

The gentlemen had remained close over the intervening years. Along with Simon and Nicholas. Or as close as Robert would allow, in any case.

Contrary to Robert's desperate attempts to distance himself from his three friends, the tragedy that had befallen Gina had sealed their fates. Simply put, living through such an ordeal had created a bond that even Robert's best attempts could not break.

After Gina's death, Robert had barely spoken to any of them. Yet when he'd returned to Eton, every day they were at his door, dragging him into life again. At Oxford, they had done the same. And when they'd each ascended to their titles—two dukes, a marquess, and an earl—they'd reached an unspoken agreement not to speak of the tragedy.

It was the only reason Robert remained friends with them. And though he rarely, if ever, admitted it, their friendship had been the only thing that had kept him alive all those years ago. And he was grateful for it. Then and now.

Though the young men didn't see each other often, he knew that James had continued to be quite sickeningly *good* throughout his life. A paragon the matrons of the *ton* flung their daughters at with abandon and debutantes simpered and swooned about.

Nicholas, too, had grown to become a favourite of Society. Though the main seat of his duchy was in Ireland, he spent almost all of his time in London, even during the summer months when most people disappeared to enjoy the sunshine in their country homes or in Bath or Brighton by the sea.

Simon was, by all accounts, as debauched and rakish as he had always claimed he would be. And Robert was secretly pleased that of the four of them, he wasn't the only one with a blackened soul.

The first rays of brilliant orange began to rise over the clifftops, signalling the start of another interminable day.

Robert negated to summon his valet, preferring to dress himself.

He would ring for a pot of strong coffee and then

go for an early morning ride, careful to avoid the river as he always was.

Then he could return and wonder what on earth James could want from him.

James, he knew, was only just returning from the Americas after a prolonged stay.

He had written that he was going to break his journey with Simon in Liverpool before travelling on to visit Robert.

A swift smile once again lit Robert's face. James and Simon were a study in opposites.

If Robert was a monster then Simon, Earl of Dashford, was certainly the Devil he'd been labelled as.

Without doubt, James and Nicholas were veritable saints compared to the sinners that were Robert and Simon.

Still, Robert was the one James wanted the favour from.

Perhaps it was a sort of familial connection, though they weren't blood relatives. Perhaps it was yet another ruse of James's to surreptitiously check on him, an attempt to convince him yet again to join the land of the living.

The Season was approaching, Robert knew. Another that he ignored, wilfully abandoning his duties at Parliament.

Robert donned his charcoal grey superfine, tying his cravat haphazardly. No doubt his valet would hunt him down and fix it at some point, but for now, Robert just wanted to escape the confines of the house, which was larger than most but somehow felt oppressively small.

Making his way toward the stables, Robert acknowledged the various greetings from stable hands and grooms with a silent nod.

Nobody would ever accuse him of being friendly and chatty, but neither would he ignore hardworking members of his household.

Arriving at the stables and calling for his mount, Storm, Robert inhaled the tangy air that always held the salty reminder that he lived close to the sea.

Strangely, the unforgiving sea didn't scare him. In fact, he loved the rugged, dangerous coastline that bordered his estate. It often mirrored his mood and was a comforting reminder that he was just one, insignificant person surrounded by a huge, if unforgiving world.

The unmistakeable whinny of his black stallion snapped Robert out of his musings, and he mounted the steed before turning toward the wide expanse of fields where he could give the horse his head.

It would be some hours before James arrived, begging his favour. And with Robert's mood blacker than usual, he was inclined to refuse before he even knew what the favour was.

Chapter Two

"WELL IT IS certainly different from New York."

Abigail Langton smiled ruefully at her companion, who sat across from her in the plush carriage.

James Harring, Marquess of Avondale, smiled back at her.

"That is because we are in the wilds of Northumberland, Abby. London will be more like what you're used to, I expect."

"Yet you insist that we come here first," she countered, raising a brow slightly.

In truth, as the bustle of Liverpool, where they'd stayed a couple of days with James's friend Lord Dashford, gave way to the more rugged landscapes of the North of England, Abby felt her excitement mounting.

Now that they'd entered the county of Northumberland, she'd almost cricked her neck trying to take in the craggy beauty around her.

She'd never seen such a beautiful place in her life. It seemed to speak to her very soul.

In fact, she'd been feeling that way since they'd first docked in the country of her mother's birth.

"I did," James said stoutly, unrepentantly. "I told you, it's bad enough that we even stayed with Simon without another female in attendance. And it's positively ruinous that you travelled alone with me from America in the first place. If the *ton* finds out, your life here in England will be over before it's begun."

"And hiding me away in—what did you call it?" She frowned in confusion, and James grinned again.

"Northumberland."

"Right." Abby nodded. "Northumberland." A bit of a mouthful, but she'd get used to it. "As I was saying, hiding me away here first will mean I'm respectable?"

"I'm not hiding you away. But you cannot show up at Town for a Season without a reputable sponsor."

"And that's not you?"

James laughed.

"No, that is most certainly not me."

"But aren't you rather a big deal here? Mother said you were."

"Yes, I am. But I am also male. And single."

"And my cousin," Abby reminded him. "Practically a brother."

"How you feel about me, and I you, has very little to do with it."

Abby sighed and shook her head, dislodging a

golden blonde strand from her chignon.

The maid James had insisted on hiring for propriety's sake, who was currently sitting atop their conveyance since she didn't travel well, would be angry with her.

Abigail had yet to go an entire day without doing damage to her maid's attempts at styling her hair.

"I will never understand your stuffy customs, James."

"They're not my customs. They are the customs of the *beau monde*. And if you want to experience a London Season, which you claimed to do *loudly,* then you have to follow the rules."

"Very well," she sighed. In the next moment, however, she brightened considerably. "I don't care how I get there, as long as I get there."

James grinned indulgently.

"I'm only sorry I don't have any sisters, my dear. If I did, we could have gone directly to London and gotten you ready."

"I suppose if you're not an appropriate chaperone, then Thomas is definitely out of the question," Abby grinned.

She'd never met her cousin Thomas, James's younger brother.

And she'd only met James because he had business in New York that he'd oversee.

It had been destiny, she'd told him the day she'd

begged him to escort her back to London. The fates wanted her in England.

"The fates might," James had quipped. *"But I'm sure your parents don't."*

Abby hadn't quite known how to explain that she had been little more than a thorn in her mother's side ever since her birth.

Mrs. Langton was an inherent snob whose life's ambition was to ensure that everyone around her knew she was the epitome of high society. Blue-blooded English stock, the daughter of a marquess.

As a wilful youth, she'd found it terribly romantic to run away to America with a wealthy merchant's son.

However, it hadn't taken long for her to realise she desperately missed the rolling green hills of England and, more importantly, the sycophantic fawning that came with being the daughter of a powerful Peer.

Unfortunately for the newly-married Mrs. Langton, she had become pregnant with Abigail only months later, and her fate had been sealed.

Which was how Abby had become a source of regret and bitterness for both her parents, though her father made the effort to hide it occasionally. In her father's defence, he hadn't always been uncaring of Abigail. In truth, he'd rather doted on her in her earliest memories. But, Abby supposed that years of his wife's obvious unhappiness, and Abigail being one of the main sources of it, had worn the man down. And so it was that he had come to care as little as his wife did.

Abigail knew their disastrous history because it was one of her mother's favourite stories to tell.

"And the duchess doesn't mind sponsoring me?" Abby asked now, refusing to give her uncaring mother any more headspace.

James had told her very little, save that the dowager duchess had only a son and would benefit greatly from a young lady to go about London with.

Plus, being the particular friend of the Duchess of Montvale would open every conceivable door to her, James had said.

When she'd first put the proposal to her cousin, whom she'd only met a year ago but who had already come to be like a brother to her, he'd steadfastly refused.

There was no way he was taking her across the Atlantic with him to jolly old England. No, he didn't care that she was positively desperate for a famed English Season. No, he didn't care that she dreamed of seeing the land she read so much about in her ridiculous romantic novels. No, he didn't care that it was high time she found a husband, and that as the granddaughter and now cousin of the esteemed Marquess of Avondale, she really should marry a Peer.

And poor James had naïvely thought that was the end of the matter.

But Abby had long since had a reputation of being able to get her own way, whether through winsome smiles, pretty pouts, or good old-fashioned manipulation.

She'd engaged in all three zealously until she'd worn James down and he'd helped her convince her mother, his aunt, that it would be a good idea.

Their journey across the Atlantic had been dull as ditch water. James had barely allowed her to leave the cabin he'd procured for her. And never, ever without her maid.

It had been a long and arduous journey and not one that she relished completing.

Well, perhaps she'd fall in love with an English lord and would end up making her home here rather than make the return journey, though she couldn't imagine never seeing her sisters again.

Her poor sisters hadn't fared much better than Abby when it came to their mother's regard. She had done her duty, providing more children to her husband, though she had never managed to give him the son he so craved.

It had been left to Abigail to provide any and all real love and affection to her sisters. But they were no longer very young. In fact, Alison had already come of age, and Elizabeth wouldn't be far behind. So, much as Abby knew how terribly she would miss them, she had to think of her own future. Maybe her sisters could even visit, when she got herself settled somewhere.

Abby smiled to herself. Her mother would no doubt shake her head at her eldest daughter's romantic nonsense. And resent her even more for having the life she, herself, had thrown away.

"Not at all," James said jovially enough, though Abby thought she sensed a tightening around his mouth.

"You're sure?" she pressed.

Did he hesitate a moment? It seemed he hesitated a moment.

"Of course. Ah, we are almost here."

That sounded suspiciously like changing the subject, but Abby was suitably distracted.

She turned toward the window and gasped at the beauty of the coastline. The lush green of the verdant grass interspersed with outcroppings of rock, and stone disappeared into a vista of the startling blue of the ocean that seemed to go on forever.

"Montvale Hall is one of the most beautifully situated houses in the country," James explained. "Though "house" doesn't really do it justice."

"Is it as big as Avondale Abby?" Abigail asked.

Her younger sisters had been vastly amused to know that the seat of their cousin had the same name as their sister.

"Bigger," James said with a wry smile.

"It is very kind of the duke to allow us to impose on

him for almost four weeks," Abigail said, eyes still on the landscape.

If she had looked at James then, she would have seen him pull guiltily at his cravat.

"Well, he is family," James said, and there was that strange expression on his face again.

A prickle of unease ran along Abby's spine.

"Your family," she corrected. "Not mine. And not really, come to that. You aren't actually related."

"Nevertheless, it will be good for the dowager to have you there. He will see that."

Abigail frowned at the cryptic remark but before she could question anything else, they passed through two massive wrought iron gates and onto the long driveway toward the Hall.

She resisted the urge to stick her head out the window in order to catch a glimpse of the house.

Finally, after an age, the carriage pulled up to a circular driveway, centred by an ominous looking fountain.

Abigail felt her jaw drop at the image in front of her.

The place was a fortress, and it really did nothing for Abby's sudden unease.

Chapter Three

MONTVALE HALL WAS the biggest house she'd ever seen, and her own in New York wasn't to be sniffed at.

Whilst she stared, a host of activities went on around her. A footman darted over and opened the carriage door, placing the footsteps at the entrance, whilst other servants hurried over and began to take their trunks inside.

Abigail was slightly surprised at the lack of servants scurrying about, given the amount that Lord Dashford had kept, and his house had been considerably smaller than this one.

She said as much to James, who frowned slightly.

"The Duke keeps a small staff," he said, and Abby accepted the short and not very informative comment because she was still trying to take in the sheer enormity of the house.

Abby's maid, Bessie, dropped a quick curtsy of greeting before rushing off after Abigail's cases.

Still, Abby couldn't drag her gaze from the intimidating pile of bricks that loomed before her.

If asked to describe it, she would have said it was closer to a castle than a house. The walls were a dark grey stone, sprawled over three floors. The doors were huge, arched affairs. Abigail was only surprised there wasn't a drawbridge and moat. Why, it had turrets for heaven's sake, sticking out of either side.

The whole thing gave her a not altogether pleasant feeling.

"Abigail?"

James held out a hand, and she took it immediately, her attention still firmly on the house.

"Impressive, huh?"

Abigail spared James a quick glance.

"Just a little." She smiled ruefully. "A little frightening, even," she added.

"Not unlike its owner," James said quietly.

Abigail only had time to offer a confused frown before James's attention was caught by something at the house.

Abigail redirected her gaze, and was unable to stifle her gasp.

James's attention was caught by some*one* at the house. The handsomest someone Abigail had ever seen.

She could only watch, her cornflower blue eyes widening of their own volition, as this giant stranger marched purposefully toward them.

He must be the duke, she thought; only a man of

great power could exude it in such a way. The air around him seemed to fairly tremble with it.

The servants had all stiffened slightly when he'd appeared, as well.

Abigail's grip on James's arm tightened.

"The duke?" she asked in a trembling whisper.

"Indeed," James answered, though he didn't sound remotely affected.

Probably because he, too, was rather big, ridiculously handsome, and a powerful Peer.

It didn't seem fair to Abigail that one country should get two such men.

Then she thought back to the Earl of Dashford with whom they'd just had a fleeting stay, and she conceded that since he, too, was devilishly handsome, rich as Croesus, and a Peer, it didn't seem to be confined to just these two. Perhaps there was something in the English water to produce such men.

And clearly, men of this type stuck together.

By now, the duke had come to a stop in front of them, towering over her and ever so slightly taller than James.

It was akin to being in a land of giants.

The Duke of Montvale's eyes raked over her, setting her body alight from her blonde curls to her kid boots.

Abigail trembled and for some inexplicable reason, she felt heat climb from her neck to her cheeks.

She had the ridiculous urge to fan herself.

Gracious! What on earth was happening to her?

She allowed her own eyes to wander freely as that steely grey glare moved to James.

The duke had to be well over six feet tall. And since Abby was a diminutive five-feet-two-inches, the difference was huge.

Lord, but he was big.

Abigail had laughed when James told her of English lords' tendency to have their jackets padded in order to seem bigger and more masculine. She thought it ludicrous.

This man, however, needed no such padding. And judging from the way his dark grey superfine was moulded to him, it would be obvious if he did.

His chest was broad, his shoulders broader still. His hair was a deep, jet black and ruffed slightly in the sea breeze.

Her eyes raked greedily over him. Black breeches that strangely made her mouth dry. Shiny black Hessians.

He was the epitome of a well put together English lord.

She allowed her eyes to travel back to his face and was not only shocked but mortified to discover that he was glaring at her.

It wasn't a terribly friendly expression; his strong jaw was tight and his eyes were dark and stormy, like a winter's sky. But before she could blink, they'd returned to her cousin.

"James, it's good to see you again."

The tall, brooding duke spoke, and Abby had to fight to stifle a sigh. His voice was just as she would have imagined it to be—warm, deep, and sinful. It put her in mind of all manner of improper things.

And considering he had looked at her with nothing but disdain on his chiselled face, that was lunacy indeed.

"You know, that was almost believable," James answered, earning himself a beautiful, though fleeting smile.

"And you are not alone." The duke's wintry eyes travelled once more to Abby.

"No, I'm not." James's tone was casual and friendly, the very opposite of the duke's.

No, the duke's tone matched his expression, and it slowly dawned on Abby that this huge, taciturn man hadn't been expecting her.

She snapped her eyes to James, hoping to convey her displeasure with her fiercest scowl, but he appeared as nonchalant about her unhappiness as he was about his friend's.

"Your grace, allow me to introduce—"

"I knew you'd come back from the Americas with a tonne of money, James. But a secret wife? Isn't that more your brother's bent?"

Abby scowled at her deceitful older cousin before turning her shocked gaze to the duke. His words had just registered. *A wife?*

How ugly he made the word sound.

Once more, that steely gaze studied her, his expression bored and displeased.

"A blonde, too," he continued derisively. "I always figured you for a brunette lover."

Abby's jaw dropped at the man's rudeness.

She was mightily affronted. And, alright, she wasn't *actually* James's wife. But this brute thought she was. And if she *were* James's wife, this would be an abominable way to be treated.

Brunette, indeed. Her bright hair had always been one of her only redeeming qualities, or so said Mrs. Langton.

While she stewed, the duke bowed respectfully as though he hadn't just been unpardonably rude to her.

She dipped a curtsy automatically, all the while wishing James and his horrible friend to Perdition.

"How do you do, Lady Avondale?"

He didn't sound as though he cared a whit how she did.

"Very well, your grace." She beamed at him, saccharinely sweet. "And you?"

If she'd been hoping to dazzle him with her smile, it would seem she was to be disappointed, for his stoic expression remained unmoved.

The mere raise of a brow was enough to signal his displeasure, and he ignored her question completely. Some imp of mischief, one that had gotten her into countless amounts of trouble, awoke in her.

"Your journey was a pleasant one, I hope."

"About as pleasant as you are finding this visit I'd imagine, your grace," she answered boldly.

Her words seemed to freeze the very air around them.

Even the horses that had pulled their carriage grew stock still.

But before Abby had time to berate herself, James's bark of laughter filled the silence, and Abby found herself able to breathe again.

Lord Montvale did not laugh, however. No, he merely scowled once more before turning on his heel and marching back to the house.

James took Abby's hand and placed it in the crook of his arm, and they made their way to the house at a slower pace.

"You didn't tell him I was coming," Abby whispered furiously.

"No, I didn't," James answered far too casually for Abby's liking.

"He thinks I'm your wife," she continued.

"Yes, he does."

"I'm not wanted here, James."

"No," he agreed, insultingly fast. "But you are

needed here."

Abby didn't respond as she stepped over the threshold and into the cavernous darkness of Montvale Hall.

"IT'S OUT OF the damned question. And you're out of your damned mind."

Robert didn't even attempt to control his temper as he sloshed several fingers of brandy into a glass, petulantly refusing to fill one for his oldest friend.

James seemed unconcerned however, and moved to stand by Robert and fill his own tumbler.

"I knew you wouldn't be happy, but—"

"Unhappy doesn't even begin to cover it. You had no right to foist yourself on me for four weeks. And you had even less right—" Robert's voice grew louder as James opened his mouth to interrupt. "—to bring some little American termagant with you."

"You don't even know her."

"I know enough."

"You know enough? After approximately five minutes in her company?"

Robert clenched his teeth at James's scoffing.

Yes, he knew enough.

He knew that girl was trouble. Knew it when his eyes had raked greedily over her of their own volition.

When something stirred to life inside him as he took in her slender frame encased in the blue velvet of her carriage dress. When he'd seen the mischief sparkle in those impossibly blue eyes of hers.

And when his breath caught as the sun glinted off her golden curls.

And he especially knew it when she'd opened that mouth and spoken so boldly, so cheekily.

So, he chose to ignore his body's immediate reaction to her and instead focused on her daring and uncouth manners, her distinct lack of proper behaviour. He'd never considered himself overly pious but really, he'd grown used to people being in awe of him. Afraid, even. If not by him then certainly by the title of duke.

And here was this doll-like hoyden who *teased* him, for God's sake. Him!

And now James expected the chit to stay here. It was the outside of enough.

When James had explained that she wasn't his wife and was, in fact, his younger, very much unattached cousin, Robert had felt a relief unlike anything he'd ever known surge through him. And on its heels, a panicked anger. For if she were not married to his friend, that meant there was nothing to stop him from pursuing her if he chose to give in to this unwanted attraction, which he absolutely did not want to do.

He couldn't, wouldn't, have that.

"I have no desire to spend more than five minutes in her company," Robert said, realising that James had been studying him during his musings.

"And what of the duchess?"

It was asked quietly enough, but it echoed loudly in Robert's head.

What of his mother? Would she want Miss Langton's—not Lady Avondale's—company? Enjoy it?

Lord knew, when she met the blonde inconvenience, the duchess had produced the first real smile Robert had seen from her in years.

"My mother hasn't been interested in the Season in years, James. What makes you think she'll want to sponsor some nobody from the Americas?"

Robert watched in a sort of perverse amusement as James's blue eyes flashed with anger.

"A little respect when you speak of my cousin, Montvale," his friend said quietly yet tersely.

Though Robert didn't feel the slightest bit intimidated, he realised it was in both of their interests to let the matter drop.

James didn't lose his temper often, which made the affable marquess quite the force to be reckoned with when he was angered.

And though Robert wasn't a bit cowed by this display of James's displeasure, he also had no desire to truly upset his friend.

"My apologies." He bowed slightly, knowing full

well he didn't sound remotely apologetic.

James's raised brow said he knew it, too.

"Abby is... unconventional in ways," James allowed.

Unconventional? Ha! It was all Robert could do to keep his countenance. Mere moments in the girl's presence, and Robert could tell James would have his work cut out for him if he were to escort the girl for a Season.

"But she is an innocent, and I'm determined she stays that way."

"And this is my problem, how?" Robert asked.

"It's not," James conceded. "But I can't very well parade around London with a single woman, can I? The matriarchs of the *ton* won't care that Abby is akin to a sister to me. They'll tear her apart like the vultures they are."

"Indeed," Robert agreed with James, for it was the truth. "But she is American. Should she face any scandal, she can just go home. In fact, why *is* she here? Surely New York has enough society of its own?"

"Not enough to satisfy Abby's penchant for romance, apparently. It seems that years of reading ridiculous novels has put the idea of some English lord or other in her head. And she's determined to meet some."

Christ, she sounded even more annoying than he'd first feared.

There was no way she was staying here. And that was that.

"WHY, OF COURSE you are staying here, my dear. It is so *good* to have you, and I cannot tell you how excited I am at the thought of sponsoring you for a Season."

Robert gritted his teeth and pointedly ignored James's smug grin.

It seemed that his friend, soon to be former friend if he kept grinning so, had been right. The dowager duchess looked as though she were coming back to life. And all because of the American chit who looked like an angel sitting across the dinner table.

"Mother, I didn't think you had an interest in going to Town," he said gruffly.

He hated to kill even a tiny amount of pleasure for his mother, but the idea of escorting ladies to London and then around to various events for the Season was anathema to him.

"Well, we can't very well let Miss Langton go alone, Robert." His mother smiled indulgently at the blonde temptress, even if she was an unwitting one. "And it can hardly be left to James alone to escort her. Besides, she needs a sponsor, and having the patronage of a duchess will help to secure her standing."

"It all sounds a little daunting, your grace." Miss

Langton returned his mother's smile, and Robert pointedly ignored the dimples that appeared on either side of her pink lips.

Dimples, for God's sake. She may as well be made of china.

They'd eat her alive in London.

"You will be just fine, my dear," his mother said kindly. "Now, we have a lot of work to do before we are to travel to London. So, I think—"

Robert ceased paying attention as his mother began to talk about a plethora of inane and expensive-sounding rules and activities.

"Look how happy she is." James leaned across to whisper to Robert.

"Shut up, James." Robert scowled.

The chattering from the females was interspersed with little giggles and sighs from Miss Langton, which darkened Robert's mood further still.

This was going to be a very long four weeks.

Chapter Four

ROBERT SIGHED AS the silence cloaked him in a welcoming embrace.

Over the last few days, his mother had turned his household upside down.

No, not his mother. Miss Abigail Langton with her blonde curls and her sky-blue eyes and her annoying habit of smiling all the damn time.

It had snuck up on him, he admitted to himself, this infiltration of his estate.

And apparently, it was getting worse.

Robert walked into the breakfast parlour and stopped dead at the sight before him.

There, in the middle of the table, stood an enormous vase positively bursting with wildflowers.

Flowers. On *his* table.

He'd never had flowers on his bloody table. Not since—well, he just didn't have them.

"Barton," Robert called for his longstanding and ever-present butler.

And as expected, the older gentleman appeared as if from nowhere, gliding into the room as though he were on wheels.

"What is this?" Robert bit out.

"Your grace?"

"This—" Robert waved his hand impatiently at the offending vase.

The butler glanced in the direction of Robert's waving hand then back at the young master.

"Tis a vase, your grace," he answered evenly.

Barton never expressed emotion or opinion. Not through language, facial expression, or tone.

And yet, Robert couldn't help but feel that the response was slightly sarcastic.

He pinched the bridge of his nose. He'd had a damned headache since the chit's arrival. And even when he'd done all he could to avoid her, her *presence* was just everywhere.

It was bloody vexing.

"I know it's a vase," he answered through gritted teeth. "But where did the flowers come from, and why the hell is it in the middle of my table?"

"Good morning, your grace."

Barton was saved from answering by the arrival of the woman herself.

Robert turned to face her with his most fearsome scowl and was rewarded by a slight widening of her eyes and a definite dimming of her smile.

He surprised himself with a tiny twinge of guilt. But of course, that was ridiculous. He was just tired.

Why should he care that he'd potentially hurt her feelings?

When Robert didn't respond, Abigail turned to Barton.

"Good morning, Barton," she said sweetly, her smile firmly back in place.

"Good morning, Miss Langton."

Barton, the traitor, provided a rare smile of his own for the young lady.

"A pot of tea, miss?"

"Coffee, please," she answered, to Robert's surprise. His mother wouldn't be caught dead drinking the stuff, though he preferred it himself in the mornings. But then, this girl was American. And clearly wasn't given to any sort of proper behaviour.

No, that was unfair, Robert had to admit to himself grudgingly, as he moved to take his place at the head of the table.

Although Miss Langton smiled far too often and laughed heartily instead of giggling in that breathless, irritating way that debutantes did, she hadn't ever displayed vulgar or scandalous behaviour. And while she was a little hoydenish, never shying away from robust conversation for example, she wasn't shocking.

Besides, his mother couldn't have approved more if the girl had been escorted here by Prinny himself.

The dowager was well and truly enamoured of the unwanted bundle of blonde who was now seating herself to his right.

Robert sat after she did. He must remember his manners, after all.

"What do you think of the flowers, your grace?" Miss Langton asked in that lilting voice that a lesser man probably would have found endearing.

He wasn't a lesser man.

"I don't have flowers on my tables," he answered gruffly before lifting his morning paper and blocking her from his view.

Was he disappointed that he could no longer see her face? Her cornflower-blue eyes?

Of course not!

"Well, you do now," she answered with a laugh and shockingly unfazed by his frown that had grown men trembling in their boots. "I was taking a walk toward the village yesterday, and I came across a field positively teeming with the most beautiful flowers, so I decided to pick some for your mother, since she is so fond of lavender. They must grow here in abundance given how close to the coast you are."

Robert slowly lowered his paper, half annoyed, half astonished.

Had she even taken a breath yet?

From the corner of his eye he saw Barton enter again, followed by most of his staff of footmen and maids, who set about placing dishes on the sideboard.

And damned if the old codger wasn't smiling.

He must find this vastly amusing. Robert did not.

He liked peace and quiet in the morning. Now it felt as though he'd been invaded by a tiny, twittering bird.

"So, anyway, I had to dash back to the Hall to grab a basket because, of course, I couldn't carry armfuls of lavender back. And then I realised I hadn't actually seen any flowers around the place. And tis a wonderful season for them, being spring and all."

She cut herself off to smile her thanks at a footman who poured coffee into a delicate china cup in front of her and earned herself a heated blush from the lad.

It seemed, however, that Miss Langton had no idea the effect she had on the men around her, for she rabbited on oblivious.

"It only took four trips and eight baskets, but I managed to fill vases for here, your mother's drawing room, the dining hall, and your mother's bedchamber. And mine, of course."

Surely his heart hadn't picked up speed at the mention of the lady's bedroom.

What the hell was wrong with him?

"I would have filled one for your room, too. And James encouraged me to."

Robert would just bet he did.

"But you didn't strike me as the type of man who'd like a vase of flowers in your room. Besides, I hardly thought you'd want me in your bedchamber."

Robert froze as a spark of lust ignited inside him at her innocent words.

He could do nothing but stare at his unwanted companion, while his mind unexpectedly conjured all sorts of reasons for her to be in his bedchamber.

And while he stared, he saw the exact moment that she realised what she'd said.

Her wide eyes widened further still, and a delicate blush stained her cheeks.

"Oh dear," she mumbled before biting her lip and making the situation much, much worse.

"I don't want your damned flowers in my bed-chamber or anywhere else in the house," he snapped, earning himself a look of hurt and a twist in his gut.

Before she inadvertently did or said anything else to loosen Robert's ever tenuous grip on his control, the door flew open and James entered.

It seemed Robert was well and truly not to have his solitude this morning, yet he found himself relieved beyond words that his friend had joined them.

"Good morning, Abby. Morning, Robert."

James swept into the room and immediately moved to the sideboard and the as yet untouched food.

Abigail immediately moved to join him, darting a quick, embarrassed look at Robert before she stood.

Robert sighed his frustration. Something had just happened here; something had awoken inside him and would not be repressed. But he had neither the time nor the inclination to try to figure it out.

If his mother was going to insist on going to Town for the Season, then he needed to get out onto his estate with his steward and make plans for his absence.

He could refuse to join the party heading to London, of course.

His mother hardly needed an escort, and James would be with them, besides.

But for the first time in years, his mother had a real smile on her face and was enthusiastic about something. Robert didn't want to take that away from her in any way. Especially considering he was to blame for her ever-present sadness.

His heart twisted in the familiar, painful way as his guilt momentarily took hold.

It would perhaps do him some good to see his mother enter Society and the land of the living again.

And he'd get to spend some time with not only James, but Nicholas and Simon, too, since they'd all be in Town together.

At the idea of the young, innocent Miss Langton being in the clutches of Simon or in the thrall of Nicholas, Robert's mood suddenly darkened even further than it already was.

Oh, he was going to London. And he would be by Miss Langton's side for the duration.

For much as he had no desire to act as a nanny for the girl, there was no way in hell he would allow Simon to get his hands on her.

And he refused to examine why that was.

Chapter Five

ABIGAIL WATCHED IN shock as the duke swept from the room without a word or even a look in either hers or James's direction.

James had described the duke as quiet, brooding, even occasionally gruff.

But he had never mentioned the young duke's overt rudeness and unbearable sulkiness.

And yet, every time he locked those sinful, stormy grey eyes on her, she felt her heartrate pick up alarmingly.

Abby had never had such a wanton, but entirely unwanted, reaction to a man. Why, he was a positive brute!

So why then, had she become breathless when he'd gazed at her as she'd stupidly talked about being in the man's bedchamber?

Her mouth often ran away from her but really, to speak to the man about such things. She mightn't understand the countless rules and regulations of London Society, but even she knew speaking of such things wasn't exactly ladylike.

And the visions she had of what he might *do* in that bedchamber. Well, that was *definitely* not ladylike.

"His bark is worse than his bite."

James's voice by her ear caused Abby to jump and pulled her immediately from her wicked contemplations.

Gracious, the duke would distract a saint.

"Is it?" she asked wryly, with a raise of her brow.

James laughed as he took his seat across from her.

"Well, probably not, no."

"I wonder that he can retain any staff, if his reputation is true."

"What reputation?" James asked.

"In the village. Did you know they call him the Monster of Montvale Hall?"

"Listening to gossip, little cousin?" James raised his own brow.

And Abby felt immediately ashamed.

"It's hard not to," she defended herself. "As soon as the locals heard I was staying here, they positively yelled it at me."

James made a noise of annoyance.

"The locals have too much time on their hands," he scoffed. "Robert is no monster. And he treats his staff very well, Abby."

She was shamed once more by the tone of admonishment in James's speech.

"They spoke of a tragedy," she said hesitantly.

Abby didn't want to pry, of course, and she would never ask the dowager anything that might hurt the dear lady.

And she would never be brave enough to ask the duke. So she was asking James, even knowing that he didn't approve of her gossiping.

"I'm sure they did," James answered with a frown. "There was a tragedy. A terrible, awful tragedy. But it's not my story to tell."

"Though you were here for it," Abby pressed on relentlessly.

"And how do you know that?"

"The—"

"The locals," James finished for her. "It would answer all of them better to keep their mouths shut."

Abby was surprised by the seriousness in James's face and tone; he was always so jovial.

"And they spoke so highly of you," she quipped, hoping to lighten the mood.

"They did?" he asked, surprised.

"Of course! The Angel of Avondale."

James scowled at the title, but his blue eyes were alight with humour once again.

"Poetic lot, aren't they?"

Abby laughed, glad the tense atmosphere between them seemed to have dissipated.

She didn't want to be at odds with James. She only wished she could keep her mind from his brooding friend and the mystery he presented.

"Are you ready for our ride?" James asked, now that he'd eaten his fill.

"I am. I shall change directly."

James had promised to take her for a ride around the estate that he knew as well as his own.

Abby loved to ride and had a great seat. She'd been itching to traverse the sweeping estate, especially the coastline. Perhaps even wander onto the beach, dip her toes in the cold Atlantic waters.

"I'll wait for you by the stables," James said and stood as Abby took her leave and dashed off to her rooms.

The dowager had already given leave for Abby to spend the morning riding, citing busyness in getting ready to open the duke's townhouse in Mayfair and packing for a Season.

Abby couldn't imagine what the older woman would want to pack, considering their first order of business when they got to London would be to go directly to a mantua maker for dresses for their stay.

Abby had assured the dowager that her dresses were fine. The dowager, with a steely eye, had assured Abby they were not.

Which was presumably why James had insisted on having the lady's guidance when it came to Abby's entrance to Society.

The good news about the dowager's insistence on a

new wardrobe was that Abby could use her new riding habit that she'd brought from America now, instead of waiting until they arrived in London.

Her maid, Bessie, had already taken the garment off to be pressed that morning and when Abby returned to her rooms, it was laid out for her, and Bessie was just placing Abby's riding boots on the Aubusson carpet.

"Ah there you are, miss. I was just finishing up."

"Thank you, Bessie." Abby smiled her appreciation at her maid and confidante.

"You'll look so fetching in this colour, Miss Abby," Bessie said.

The habit was a crushed velvet of midnight blue that made her eyes seem startling in their colour and was a perfect foil for her bright, blonde hair.

She allowed Bessie to help her into the heavy skirt and fitted jacket, then stood still whilst the young girl painstakingly closed the row of tiny black buttons.

Finally, a dainty hat of the same blue with a small black feather was affixed to her head.

"Pretty as a picture, miss." Bessie smiled, and Abigail returned the grin.

Making her way downstairs, Abby was battling a stubborn button on her black riding gloves when her over-long riding skirt got tangled in her feet.

With a gasp, she reached out to gain purchase on the bannister but missed.

This is going to hurt, she thought in the seconds

before she went tumbling down the stairs.

But just as she tipped forward, a strong hand grabbed her around the upper arm and pulled her back to safety.

Breathless, Abigail turned to face her rescuer and was met with the black scowl of her disobliging host.

"Y-your grace," she stuttered, heart still hammering, though that could be because he was still holding her and she could feel the heat of his grip even through her layers of clothing.

Abigail gazed up, trapped in eyes the colour of a winter sky.

"Thank you."

Lord Montvale said nothing. Simply stared at her with the oddest look on his darkly handsome face, his eyes growing even stormier.

Though he towered over her already, the fact that she was two stairs below made him positively loom over her.

And although it made him even more intimidating than usual, Abby found herself not afraid, but excited.

Something dark, and wicked, and thrilling unfurled in her belly as she met his stare with her own.

"I—"

Before she could speak another word, the mysterious emotion that had darkened his gaze disappeared and in its place were freezing chips of grey ice.

"Why don't you bloody well look where you are

going?" he hissed, his anger evident and shocking.

"I'm s-sorry," Abby began to stutter before clamping her mouth shut.

Her own anger flared as though he'd lit a match to it.

What was she apologising for? For almost killing herself on his stupid staircase?

Perhaps he didn't want her here, but it was James who'd brought her. It wasn't as though she'd appeared on his doorstep by herself.

And the dowager had assured her more than once that she was enjoying having Abby around.

Montvale Hall was huge! The biggest building she'd ever been in, so it wasn't that she was underfoot.

No, she wasn't anywhere inconvenient enough to warrant this behaviour from him. And she'd had enough.

"Actually," she said, as he dropped her arm and turned on his heel to march back up the stairs, "I take that back."

The duke froze mid-step then turned slowly to face her.

"You take what back?" he asked, his jaw clenched.

"My apology." She wouldn't be deterred. Not by his tone. Not by his scowl. Not by his—well, his himness!

He frowned in confusion, and she concentrated on not being moved by the lock of dark hair that fell across his brow with the action.

"I don't apologise for nearly falling down the stairs," she continued, taking a step toward him.

"I don't apologise for James having brought me here, since I had nothing to do with it." She took another step closer.

He still seemed to stretch above her for miles, but at least she was levelling the battlefield a little.

"And I don't apologise for occasionally forcing you to spend time in my presence, loathsome as that is," she finished, almost yelling, and now just one step below him.

He didn't speak in response to her outburst, and she felt a twinge of shame at her childishness. Especially in the face of his stoicism.

His eyes made a slow perusal of her from head to toe and back again. And the look in them said he found her wanting.

"You're irritating," he said in an emotionless tone.

Abby gasped at his rudeness.

"And you," she said in a fierce whisper, her cheeks scarlet with humiliation and hurt, "are a rude, unfeeling brute."

Without giving him a chance to respond and make her feel even worse about herself, Abby turned on her heel and dashed down the stairs and out the door, barely giving the footman time to open it for her.

God, she hated him!

Monster, indeed, she fumed as she marched toward the stables. It seemed a fitting title.

Chapter Six

ROBERT LEFT HIS steward at the stables and decided to take his stallion Storm for a ride around the estate.

He'd been feeling restless all morning, and he knew the beast sensed it.

The name Storm suited the fiery, strong animal, and it gave Robert a perverse sort of pleasure to name it after the weather that had changed the course of his life forever, and that of everyone around him.

It never allowed him to be free of the memories. And the accompanying guilt was deserved and therefore welcome, even if it seemed as though it ate him alive daily.

But it wasn't his guilt about his sister at the forefront of Robert's mind that morning. It was a pair of hurt-filled blue eyes.

He'd been unpardonably rude to Miss Langton this morning, he knew.

And even as he swiftly went through the estate business with his steward, riding out to a tenant's cottage to see some mild damage to the roof and ordering said damage to be fixed immediately, he couldn't shake the feeling of remorse gnawing at him.

His mother would have his head should Miss Langton tell tales. And why shouldn't she? He'd been as boorish as his reputation allowed.

Plus, the chit was right. It wasn't actually her fault that she was here at all.

Nor was it her fault that when he'd seen her almost fall down the stairs, a fear unlike any he'd felt in years clawed at him.

And he could hardly blame her that even that merest touch, standing in such close proximity, watching the emotions flit across those incredible eyes, the plumpness of her pink lips as she'd breathed her thanks, set off a flame of desire that almost incinerated him.

Robert lost his train of thought as his mind went to the same place that had been keeping him up at night since Abigail Langton had invaded his home with that disarming smile, carrying her intoxicating floral scent everywhere she went. And filling his damned house with flowers that somehow reminded him of her.

And this thought served to remind him just why he wanted Abigail to keep her distance.

She was light and pure, beautiful and innocent. His darkness would consume her.

She was the sun in springtime. He was a wintry storm.

His entire household was brighter for her presence; the servants smiled and hummed when they thought he wasn't listening; his mother seemed decades younger.

Every once in a while, he even felt some part of himself try to pull him toward her light. And not the part that usually governed his actions when it came to a beautiful woman.

No, this was a long-deadened organ that reacted to Abigail Langton in a way that shocked and terrified him.

Last night at dinner, she'd regaled them with tales of her exploits on the other side of the Atlantic.

His mother had actually laughed aloud. And the sound was so wonderful, brought back such memories, that Robert's heart twisted painfully, even as it lifted.

James, too, had been highly amused.

"No wonder my poor aunt sent you to London with me," he'd laughed. "She couldn't control you."

And it was true. By the sounds of things, Abigail Langton was a veritable termagant. She would doubtless be a handful for whatever lord she landed in the marriage mart.

Robert felt his scowl deepen of its own accord at the idea of her meeting and marrying someone else.

Why on earth should it bother him so? It was a disturbing thought and not one he wanted to pursue.

Robert wasn't used to feeling so unsettled, and he

didn't relish the feeling.

"That behaviour will cause you untold trouble in Town, Miss Langton. There are standards here that must be adhered to."

His words had brought an immediate cessation to the joviality around the table.

As he'd watched the reaction of his friend; anger, his mother; disappointment, and the nuisance herself; embarrassment, a flicker of guilt tried to make itself known. But he'd quashed it as easily as he had quashed nearly all his emotions since his childhood.

Robert muttered an oath, shaking his head to clear it of his obsessive thoughts about Abigail Langton.

He waited impatiently for the groom to give Storm a quick rubdown before re-saddling the beast and taking off as fast as his formal gardens would allow.

Once he arrived at the outer reaches of the estate close to the cliffs, Robert gave Storm his head, hoping that the lightning speed and stiff breeze would be enough to clear his thoughts.

There was a hidden, sandy pathway down to the beach a little further on. Robert often took it and sat down on the waterfront, sometimes for hours.

The ocean didn't hold the horror of Montvale's river for Robert. The roiling sea and stark cliff edges suited his mood and were a balm for his blackened soul.

They perhaps didn't afford him any real peace but

at least a measure of it.

Not many people knew about the path either, which was another reason he craved it. Only his mother, his friends, and some long-serving servants.

It was the perfect place to go and feel miserable by himself when he tired of feeling miserable in company.

He led Storm to the entrance of the pathway, and the horse gingerly picked his way down, well used to the oft trodden path.

The spring sun was high and bright in the sky, and a swift breeze swirled around him, filling his senses with the salty tang of sea air.

Here, he could forget Miss Abigail Langton and the confusing array of emotions she awoke in him.

Here, he could ignore the dread that filled him at the thought of spending months in the jovial, glittering world of the *haute ton.*

Here, he didn't have to pretend that he wasn't the monster he'd been named as by the people who only knew what he'd become after Gina's death.

He awaited the visceral tug of pain as soon as he thought of his sister and was unsurprised when it came.

Storm had reached the compacted sand of the isolated beach, and Robert swiftly dismounted, not bothering to tether his mount.

This cove was impassable on either side, surrounded as it was by outcroppings and caves in the cliffs.

Robert gazed unseeing toward the ocean.

Thoughts of Gina had infiltrated his mind, and he knew there would be no escaping them.

It had always been thus in the lead up to the anniversary of her death.

This year, he knew, would be harder still.

For even as his mother prepared Miss Langton for a Season, even as he grudgingly agreed to escort her from one interminable event to another, in his blackened heart, he knew that everyone would be thinking the same thing; it should have been Gina.

Robert issued a string of black curses. There wouldn't be even the semblance of peace today. His thoughts were firmly fixed on his sister and his responsibility for her death.

And nothing would distract him from them.

"Steady, boy. Steady—oh, dear."

The unexpected sound of a female voice had Robert whipping around in time to see the bane of his existence, Miss Abigail bloody Langton, being unceremoniously dumped on her admittedly delectable backside by her fractious mount.

The white gelding spared his rider a dismissive whinny before trotting toward Storm.

Robert's heart slammed against his chest as he watched her fall, but even as he rushed toward her, she was climbing to her feet.

"Gracious," she said breathlessly, as she frantically

brushed the sand from her skirts. "I don't think Lancelot likes the beach."

Now that he knew she was all right, Robert felt able to feed his anger at once again having his peace shattered by the irritating miss who plagued him.

"What are you doing here?" he snapped through gritted teeth.

To his shock, she stopped her ministrations to her skirts and rolled her eyes at him.

Him! Robert Forsythe.

People did not roll their eyes at the Monster of Montvale Hall.

"Don't tell me—I'm not allowed on your beach?" She dimpled, wholly unconcerned by the daggers he was shooting her with his eyes.

"How did you even find that pathway?" he demanded, ignoring her insolence.

"James and I were riding along the coastline, and he showed it to me. But when we arrived at the path, he remembered an urgent letter he needed to send to his man of business."

"He left you on a steep cliff face by yourself?"

Robert could hear the growl in his voice, and she noticed it, too, if the widening of her impossibly blue eyes was anything to go by.

"Well, y-yes," she stuttered hesitantly. "But I am perfectly capable of—"

"You do not know the area, Miss Langton," he bit

out. "You could have come to real harm."

He was holding on to his temper by the merest thread. He could kill his friend for endangering this woman.

Robert had no idea where this animalistic protectiveness had come from. And he didn't enjoy the emotion.

But the idea of her body lying broken and bruised at the bottom of the cliffs…

He closed his eyes as the image turned his blood cold.

"Are you well?"

Her voice brought his attention snapping back to her.

With eyes filled with concern, she lifted a small hand and pressed it against his forehead.

"You've gone terribly pale."

Robert flinched away from her touch, earning himself another damned look of hurt.

But the contact was shocking in its unexpectedness. As was his reaction to it.

Robert had by no means lived as a monk.

He had a longstanding arrangement with a mistress in London for when he was forced to be in Town for business, and he'd had his fair share of affairs over the years.

But he never allowed intimacy outside of the bedchamber. Never.

And for this incorrigible chit to be touching him, burning his skin even through the buttery soft leather gloves she wore.

Well, it was enough to bring him to the brink of losing control.

He clasped her wrist, gently but firmly, and removed her hand from his head.

"I don't like company," he answered shortly.

Rather than scare her away, however, his statement earned him a dazzling smile. Complete with those dimples she had the nerve to distract him with.

"Really? I'm shocked to hear it," she answered cheekily.

He refused to react to her outrageous retort.

Even as his lips tried to twitch with amusement.

Abigail watched him through narrowed eyes before sighing, seemingly in defeat.

"If I promise not to touch, speak to, or in any way impress upon you, can I stay? I love the ocean. I love the beach. I just want to enjoy it awhile."

She was gazing at him imploringly. And as he watched her, the breeze caught a curl of golden hair and whipped it across her cheek.

Robert found himself clenching his fists to stop from reaching for that silky strand, from rubbing it between his fingers and feeling what was sure to be satiny smoothness.

"Your grace?"

Her voice once again snapped him to attention.

What the hell is wrong with you?

"Fine," he answered, desperate to put some much-needed space between them. "Just stay out of my way."

Without awaiting a response, he turned on his heel and stomped off toward the cliffs.

To leave now would be petulant, and he'd be damned if he let a tiny miss with a big mouth run him off his own beach.

He wanted quite desperately to turn back to look at her, but once again his iron self-control allowed him to keep walking away from her. And it was a good thing, too. For both their sakes.

ABIGAIL FROWNED AT the retreating back of the Duke of Montvale.

The man was a walking conundrum.

His rudeness was truly breath-taking, yet it did not offend her now as it had at first.

For standing so close to him, close enough to see the desolation in those wintry grey eyes, she knew that his behaviour came from a place of unimaginable pain.

And rather than feel anger toward him, she felt a desperate sadness, and a yearning, inexplicable need to help.

Help, she was quite sure, would be as unwelcome as

her presence here on this beach.

Sighing from the depths of her soul, Abigail turned her attention from the tall, solid, frankly mouth-watering sight of his retreating back, and took in the rest of her surroundings.

Turning her face skywards, Abigail shielded her eyes from the sun and studied the awe-inspiring cliffs rising above her.

The distant cries of soaring gulls battled with the crash of the surf, and Abby watched the wheeling specs of white as they dipped and flew around the clifftops.

Life, she decided, would be infinitely better as a bird. Birds didn't have to continually pit their wills against implacable dukes.

Nor, she was certain, did they continually want to *kiss* those same implacable dukes.

Not that a seagull could kiss, of course…

Smiling at her own silliness, she stepped back to better take in the sheer size of the cliffs before her.

She felt the shells crunch beneath her kidskin boots.

She felt the sea spray spatter across the back of her velvet habit.

She felt—

"Oof."

She felt herself slam against something hard and unyielding.

"Why are you walking backwards toward the

ocean?"

His words, spoken close to her ear, sent a delicious shiver along her neck and made her think all manner of wicked things.

How had one as large as he moved so close without making a sound?

Abby's heart fluttered, her emotions riotous.

And in her nervousness, instead of answering his question, she blurted out the first thing that came to mind.

"How do birds kiss?"

The second, the *second* she uttered the foolish question, she wished she could recall it. And the deafening silence that met her words was telling. He must think her utterly barmy.

When the silence stretched on, she gathered her courage and turned to face him.

There were mere inches between them, and Abigail had to tilt her head back to meet his shuttered stare.

His face gave nothing away and that, coupled with his proximity, made her more nervous still.

"What I mean is," she prattled on, her embarrassment loosening her tongue. "*Do* they kiss?"

Good God, Abby. Shut. Up.

"Probably not," she conceded, as if he'd been mad enough to answer her. "I-I just wondered. If they *did* kiss, how would they do it?"

Silence.

"Because they have beaks, you see."

She couldn't stop! Though an inner voice screamed itself hoarse begging her to, she could not stop the words spilling from her mouth.

"A-and, you couldn't kiss with a beak, could you? I mean, I know how humans kiss."

He raised one brow a tiny, infinitesimal amount. The only change in his impenetrable façade.

"Well, I don't *know* how humans kiss. I've never been kissed."

Abigail Marie Langton. Stop. Saying. Words.

"B-but—"

Finally, *finally* her mouth drew to a trailing halt.

Ye gads, he'll think me fit for Bedlam.

Abby sighed in a mixture of defeat and acute embarrassment.

"I just don't know how they'd do it," she mumbled lamely. "Kiss, I mean."

As if he needed or wanted clarification.

Feeling the heat of embarrassment scald her cheeks, Abby turned to move away.

Before she took one step, however, his large hand caught her upper arm.

She looked back up at him to see an unreadable expression on his face.

They stood frozen for mere seconds and yet eons

before he spoke.

"Like this," he said roughly.

And before she could speak, or even move, his other hand shot up, cupped the nape of her neck and pulled her toward him for an earth-shattering kiss.

Chapter Seven

LATER, ROBERT WOULD call himself every name under the sun for a blasted fool.

For now, however, his mind went completely blank as he tasted Abigail Langton.

The immediate lust that rampaged through him caught him unawares and for the first time in his adult life, Robert gave himself over to his feelings.

Abigail's hands pressed against his chest before gripping the lapels of his superfine.

And when she opened her mouth on a breathless moan, he thanked a god he hadn't been sure existed for the opportunity to deepen their kiss.

He delved his tongue inside her mouth to dance with her own as his hands traversed every blessed curve of the body pressed against him.

A madness unlike anything he'd ever experienced shattered his rigid self-control as he gently moved his lips from hers to travel along the long, smooth column of her throat.

Her gasps and moans of encouragement were fuel to the flame burning between them, urging him on.

She might look like an angel, but she was made for sin.

Robert moved his mouth upwards to catch a lobe in his teeth and growled with a primitive satisfaction as he elicited a sob of desire from her delectable lips.

Somewhere deep in his consciousness, he knew this was madness. Knew it was wrong.

She was an innocent, and James, or his steward, or any other number of people could come upon them.

"I have to stop," he whispered, barely recognising the agonised voice as his own.

"Don't," she implored desperately, and he was a base enough creature to feel a smug satisfaction in the response he'd awoken in her.

He had no doubt she was an innocent, but she was more of a temptress than any experienced woman he'd ever known.

With Herculean strength, Robert finally pulled himself away from her, shooting his arms out to steady her as she staggered slightly.

As though emerging from under water, Robert's senses and clarity of mind came back to him in a rush.

What the hell had he done?!

Abigail was gazing at him with something akin to wonder in the impossible blue of her eyes, and that look was enough to scare the wits out of him.

She looked so innocent. So trusting. So pure.

So utterly ravaged.

He really was the monster he'd been labelled, for even now the wickedest, most sinful lust raged through his veins.

He would take such innocence, such purity, and sully it with his darkness.

Muttering an oath as black as his soul, he dropped his hands from her body and turned away.

"Robert?"

He groaned aloud.

The sound of his given name on her lips, hesitant as it was, tried his control more than he would have thought possible.

"You need to leave," he snarled. "Now."

"Leave? But—"

He heard the crunch of shells beneath her feet as she took a step toward him and the devil take him, but he knew he would not have the strength to keep himself from reaching for her again.

He whipped back around to face her.

"You must leave. Now."

Robert didn't know if she heard the desperation in his voice. Maybe she was responding to the uncontrollable desire that was surely still burning in his eyes.

Whatever it was, she finally hearkened to his words.

He hardened himself against the tears that swam in her eyes before she turned and stumbled away from him.

He did not move, even when he heard her drag on Lancelot's reins to pull him back up the pathway to the cliffs above.

He did not move for what seemed an eternity.

And even as feelings roared and swirled inside him, on the outside he appeared the soulless, emotionless monster he had long been and was determined to remain.

ABBY FURIOUSLY BLINKED back the tears that threatened to spill.

She didn't even know why she was crying, not really.

It was a plethora of reasons—humiliation at her wantonness, the shame of his rejection, but mostly, the flaming desire for the brute that still licked at her veins.

When James had left her, assuring her it was perfectly safe and even better to traverse the rugged border of the vast estate alone, never would she have imagined that it would result in her being thoroughly ravaged by her intimidating host.

And intimidating he was.

When he had held her in his arms, she felt in him a strength of passion she never would have thought possible. He blazed with it, and she went up in smoke in the flames.

Yet he'd pushed her away so suddenly, snarled at her so viciously afterwards, it was like the man of passion and desire hadn't existed.

If not for her racing heart and bruised lips, Abby could have assumed she'd imagined the entire encounter.

That, and the seismic shift that had taken place in her very soul the second he'd touched her lips with his.

Abby was pragmatic enough to know that a kiss, even one as explosive as that one, would mean nothing to a man like the Duke of Montvale, even if she had been changed irrevocably and forever by it.

Abigail wasn't blind or deaf. She saw how the servants gazed at him. She heard the swoons in the voices of the local women, even as they claimed to fear him.

They might find him frightening, but they found him desirable, too. And that fact, coupled with the fact that he was a wealthy, obscenely handsome duke, would surely mean he had his pick of female company whenever he wanted it.

Abby scowled as jealousy unfurled inside her.

But this was no use! She couldn't, *wouldn't* develop affections for a man such as he. A monster such as he.

The stories she'd heard of his temper and treatment of those who'd wronged him.

The whispers she'd heard of the tragedy that lay over him and his home like a thick, smothering blanket.

They were enough to make her well aware of how foolish it would be to care for such a man.

Abby stumbled over the long, heavy skirt of her riding habit and cursed herself, her horse, and her tormentor to perdition.

She was too small to mount Lancelot without assistance and despite her coaxing and a heavy dose of wishful thinking, she hadn't been able to get the horse to kneel down so she could climb onto his back.

So now she faced a long and arduous trek back to the Hall with only her thoughts and an uncooperative horse for company.

The pounding of galloping hooves sounded behind her, pulling Abby from her maudlin musings.

With a hand shielding her eyes from the glaring sunlight, she watched in trepidation as Lord Montvale, for she would know those broad shoulders even from a distance, rushed toward her.

He'd had no problem getting onto his horse, she noted bitterly.

He thundered toward her and for a moment, it looked as though he would go straight past her and not stop.

But he suddenly reined in, the black stallion skidding to a halt and kicking up a flurry of sand around her skirts.

Poor Bessie would have an awful job trying to clean the garment after today's escapades.

Lord Montvale glared down at her, his molten silver eyes boring into her yet giving nothing away.

Abigail glared right back. Even though it felt as though her heart would thump its way out of her chest at any moment, she wouldn't be cowed by this man.

After an interminable silence, he spoke.

"Why are you walking?" he demanded, his tone imperious, his look severe.

He really was an ill-tempered beast.

"I like to walk," she answered mutinously.

He merely raised a brow in response. But it was enough to make her feel like a recalcitrant child.

Sighing in resignation, she waved a hand toward the gelding, who was disappointingly without telepathic abilities and therefore unable to understand her begging for cooperation.

"I couldn't get on the horse," she admitted, feeling a scalding heat rise in her cheeks.

How could he sit there conversing so tersely after what had happened between them on the beach?

Without a word, he jumped easily from his huge beast and stepped over.

Abigail couldn't contain her gasp as he stopped only inches from her.

He's going to kiss me again, she thought wildly.

And when his hands wrapped her around the waist, her lips parted of their own accord.

But he didn't kiss her.

Still in total silence, he lifted her clean off her feet, as though she weighed nothing at all, and placed her unceremoniously on the saddle of her horse.

Abby could only stare at him as he turned and climbed back atop his stallion, nodded abruptly to her, then rode away.

Urging Lancelot into a gentle pace, she set off behind him, feeling more confused than ever.

Chapter Eight

"WE SHOULD THEREFORE be ready to set off for London by the end of this month, if we are to arrive in the first weeks of the Season."

The dowager had chattered away making plans excitedly all through dinner, with James encouraging her. And it was giving Robert a blinding headache.

Miss Langton, at least, was quieter than usual.

Do not think about her, he instructed himself firmly. *Not about the feel of her lips against your own, not about the fire you discovered lurking beneath that innocent exterior, not about the feel of her soft, pliant body pressed against your own.*

"Robert, dear, is that amenable to you?"

"I couldn't care less when we go, Mother," he answered abruptly then immediately felt like a heel as hurt flashed in her eyes.

Damn and blast, he could not get a hold on his temper this evening.

But the end of the month would be the anniversary of Gina's death. Were they all going to just ignore it in favour of fancy balls and fripperies?

He already felt bad enough that he'd been distracted from remembering his little sister by the doe-eyed blonde driving him insane with desire.

It was annoying him that they were all seemingly ignoring Gina's upcoming anniversary, but he had caused his mother enough pain to last a thousand lifetimes already, and snapping at her was unfair and uncalled for.

"My apologies," he uttered coarsely. "What I mean is, I will ensure everything is in place for whenever you want to set off. My man of business will begin making enquiries at the inns we intend to stop at along the way."

The journey to London would take a goodly time, and the dowager would tire easily.

James, he knew, would spend as much of the journey as possible on horseback, as would he.

And as for Miss Langton, well she'd managed to cross the Atlantic, then travel from Liverpool to Northumberland after only a couple of days' rest and still look beautiful. So, she obviously travelled well.

His mother's smile returned at once.

"Thank you, dear," she said. "I know the idea of being in Town for the Season holds no appeal for you."

"Then he shouldn't come."

In shock, Robert looked down the table to the bloody nuisance with the big mouth.

As he watched, he saw the exact moment she realised that she'd been heard.

Her wide blue eyes grew larger still, and she clamped a hand over the mouth that had tormented his thoughts since he'd tasted it that morning.

A quick glance at the other occupants showed they were as shocked as he; though James looked more amused than anything else.

Robert looked back at Miss Langton and raised a brow.

His lips twitched infinitesimally in amusement as heat suffused her cheeks.

"I'm so sorry," she finally blurted into the shocked silence. "That was unpardonably rude. I-I didn't mean—that is to say... I wasn't saying..."

She floundered desperately, and Robert found himself actually feeling sorry for her. Wanting to jump in and rescue her somehow. So, of course, he stayed quiet.

Because it wouldn't do to feel anything for the chit, sympathy or otherwise.

"What I meant was that if his grace finds London so unpleasant, I should hate to be an inconvenience to him in forcing him to go."

She addressed this to her plate, presumably because she didn't dare make eye contact with any of them.

"You're already an inconvenience, Miss Langton, so it makes no difference if that's here or in London."

Once again, the room fell into a stunned silence.

This time, however, the disapproval came off his fellow occupants in waves. He didn't need to look at them to know they were furious.

Besides, his sole focus was on the beauty sitting down the table from him.

Her eyes flashed a sudden, blue fire, and an answering flame flickered to life inside him.

He'd felt more riotous emotion in the short time she'd been here than in his whole life.

It was irritating as hell. But, though he hated to admit it, there was a small part of him, a part he thought had died all those years ago on the riverbank, that found it exciting.

However, if he was hoping for a fight, he was to be disappointed it seemed.

For as closely as he was studying her, he saw the fire die in her eyes just as quickly as it had flashed there.

"I find I have a sudden headache," she mumbled into the strained silence. "Please, excuse me."

"Abigail!" his mother called after the young lady as she dashed from the room.

And James, who had stood when Abigail had, turned to face Robert, fury stamped on his usually affable face.

"What the hell is wrong with you?" he yelled.

It was a testament to his friend's anger that he

would use such language in front of the dowager.

Robert laughed, but there was no humour in it.

"Do you want a list?" he asked sardonically.

"I knew you wouldn't exactly be the most welcoming of hosts, Robert. And I know the image you so carefully cultivate so that you can hide behind it, but I've never known you to be intentionally cruel."

"Watch yourself, James," he warned, injecting steel into his voice.

He and James could say a lot of things to each other. As could Simon and Nicholas. But some things were too close to the mark, and therefore off-limits.

"Watch myself? Do you expect me to sit here and listen to you insult my cousin?"

And just like that, Robert's temper exploded.

"Why the hell shouldn't you?" he demanded, standing with enough force to send his chair tumbling to the floor. "I've had to sit here listening to you all making plans to take London by storm and ignore the anniversary of Gina's death."

His mother flinched as though he'd slapped her, and James's face blanched as he sank back in his chair with a thump.

But Robert didn't care.

His breathing was ragged, and he struggled to get it back under control.

Suddenly the room felt oppressive, the air toxic.

He turned and stormed away from them, needing

to escape their stares.

If only it were as easy to escape himself.

THE CLOCK ON the mantle ticked a steady rhythm, the only sound in the study aside from an occasional crackle of the fire.

It had been two hours since Robert had stormed from the dining room, yet he still felt as unsettled as ever.

What he'd said about Gina—it had been unspeakably cruel, he knew.

He'd never spoken like that to or in front of his mother.

And he could admit to himself, at least, that the longer he spent in the company of Miss Abigail Langton, the looser his grasp on his emotions became.

She wasn't to blame for his behaviour, of course. She wasn't to blame for his temper, or his rudeness, or his cruelty to his family and closest friend.

But the truth was the more time he spent around her, the harder it was to keep his distance. He was concentrating so much effort on not touching her as he wished or caring for her as he was afraid he could, that he was losing control in other aspects of his life.

A soft knock sounded on the closed study door, and Robert's heart picked up speed in response.

Ridiculous to think his thoughts had somehow conjured her.

"Enter," he called gruffly.

The door creaked open. But it was his mother, not Abigail Langton, who stepped hesitantly into the room.

He steadfastly ignored the twist of disappointment.

"I don't wish to disturb you."

Robert hated himself for the worry sketched on his mother's face.

When would he stop hurting this woman, whose only crime was to have given birth to him in the first place?

"You're not disturbing me," he answered softly.

He needed to apologise. But for some reason, the words stuck in his throat.

His mother moved further into the room, her burgundy skirts swishing about her as she glided forward.

Her grey eyes, a lighter shade than his own, took in her surroundings before she settled smoothly in one of the high-backed chairs and faced him.

"I used to spend so many hours in here when your father was alive," the dowager said softly, her eyes gentle, her still beautiful face etched with lines of age and grief.

"He was always so busy. Sometimes I would just sit by the window and read quietly while he worked. It was enough to be in the same room as him."

Robert felt a sickening churn of guilt and grief in

his stomach.

His father was dead because of him. The grief of Gina's death had led him to drink. And Gina's death had been Robert's fault.

"I'm sorry," he said, hearing how jagged his voice was but unable to help it. "I'm sorry for what I said at dinner. It was—unpardonable."

The dowager studied him in silence for a moment, her gaze searching.

Finally, she spoke.

"You know, there's not a day goes by that I don't think of your sister. Not one single day. Every morning I open my eyes, and for an infinitesimal moment, I forget why I feel like I can't breathe properly. And then, I remember it all."

Robert was struggling to breathe himself. He had thought he was the only one who felt that way.

But his mother had lost her child. And as torturous as his own feelings were, he couldn't even begin to imagine the horrors his mother lived with.

"The truth is, I haven't been able to take a proper breath since the day Gina died. I think it's because when you love someone as a mother loves her child, your soul splits and is no longer fully your own. Parts of it belong to your children." She paused and smiled gently at him. "And if you're lucky, to the person you marry. So, when part of your soul dies, you're never fully whole again."

His mother's words, the vocalising of her pain after all these years, were like excruciating daggers piercing Robert's heart. But he welcomed the pain. He deserved it.

"I have lost two parts of my soul."

There was a pause, a silence that Robert couldn't even attempt to fill.

"I hadn't forgotten her anniversary, Robert."

"I know," he said gruffly.

"But I can remember your sister. Grieve for her and your father, and still be among the living. I've learned that these past days."

The dowager leaned across the mahogany desk that had been his father's before him and clasped his hand.

"You haven't learned to do the same."

"That's ridiculous, I—"

"No, Robert," she interrupted softly. But it was enough to silence him because they both knew she was right.

"I don't know how." He hated himself for admitting it, a weakness in the face of his mother's unerring strength. "I don't know how you do it."

His mother shook her head sadly and squeezed the hand she still held.

"I do it because I have someone to do it for," she said. "You."

Robert's heart thumped painfully in his chest.

"So, that's the answer?" he asked, unable to keep

the bitterness from his tone. "A child?"

"Love," she answered softly, undeterred by his sneering.

He laughed derisively, hating that an image of Abigail Langton with her golden curls and wide blue eyes swam before his eyes.

"I don't have it in me to love, Mother," he said. "And who would ever love the Monster of Montvale Hall?"

"I love you," she said firmly.

Robert couldn't stand this anymore.

He pulled his hand from hers and stood.

Marching over to his steadily depleting decanter of brandy, he poured himself a generous measure and swallowed it whole.

"How can you, after what I did?"

The question tumbled from his lips before he could recall it.

He heard his mother move toward him, then felt her hand on his arm.

"You didn't *do* anything, Robert." She still spoke in that even, determined tone. A tone that almost reassured him enough to believe her. "You have to stop blaming yourself. Gina's death—"

"Was caused by me. Father's death was caused by me."

His mother blanched.

"What? *How* can you possibly think that?"

Robert shrugged her hand off his arm.

"He drank himself into an early grave, Mother, and we both know it. And he did that because he couldn't handle Gina dying. And she died *because of me.*"

Robert turned away again to stare unseeingly out his study window.

The night sky was immense and cloudless, yet the thousands of stars might well have not been there for all the attention he paid them.

He heard the dowager sigh behind him and then heard the unmistakable clink of ice hitting a glass.

Turning, he saw to his surprise that his mother was pouring an extremely generous measure of brandy for herself.

Wordlessly, she recapped the decanter, replaced it, then picked up her glass and downed the liquid in one seamless movement.

"I think," she said, turning to him, her eyes bright and fierce, "that I have made a very grave error with you, my dear."

Robert's heart stopped in his chest.

Here it came—the recrimination, the anger, the hatred he'd always expected from the only real family he had left.

Maybe their having had this conversation had woken her up to the truth of Robert's crimes.

"All these years," she continued speaking, though she made no attempt to move back to him.

And he was glad of it.

He had kept his mother at an emotional and physical distance since his childhood, he knew.

Yes, he ate meals with her, spoke to her, provided her with anything and everything he thought she could want.

But for all he cared for her, he'd treated her like a stranger at times.

So talks like these were non-existent. Until now, apparently.

Physical closeness as well as this attempt at frankness and honesty would be too much to bear.

"After Gina's death," the dowager continued, only the slight wobble in her voice indicating that her control on her emotions wasn't as strong as first appeared. "After that terrible, awful *accident*, I saw how much pain you were in. And it almost killed me, Robert."

His mother refilled her glass and then moved to sit on the chaise by the window.

Without her asking, Robert mirrored her actions and sat with his own much-needed drink.

"I will never forgive myself for allowing my own pain and grief to blind me to yours. I knew you were suffering, of course. But I-I wasn't handling things all that well at that time." She attempted a small smile but for the life of him, Robert couldn't return it. "And everyone told me that children are resilient. Children bounce back. Children accept things that adults find harder."

She stopped and took a generous gulp from her glass.

"I was selfish. So very selfish. I chose to believe what they said was true. The doctor had given me laudanum to help me sleep, and I took it for weeks, ignoring nearly everything and everyone. Pretending to myself that you didn't need more of me than the shell I was giving you."

Robert's head was spinning. How could his mother think she had *any* part in the plentiful guilt surrounding that day?

"I will never forgive myself," she spoke quietly, into her glass.

"Mother—"

"Please, let me finish," she interrupted his protestations. Reaching out and once again clasping his hand with her free hand, she continued, "Over time, it seemed as though the opportunity to truly help you come to terms with things had passed. Your nightmares had stopped."

No, they hadn't. But he'd learned to manage them alone. Pretended to everyone that they were gone.

"You remember how I used to sit with you. Sing you back to sleep."

"I remember you moved yourself into my rooms for weeks." He grinned despite the sombre mood of the evening. "If my friends at Eton had known that my mother was sleeping in a cot in my room, they'd have never let me live it down."

He was grateful to see the dowager laugh softly.

"But the nightmares stopped, and your father insisted you were ready to go back to school, and then life just seemed to…go on."

Little did his mother know that Robert had lived in a personal hell that first year back at school. And only the friendship of James, Simon, and Nicholas had kept him from something truly dire.

"I know that you blame yourself for Gina's death, despite what I have told you many, many times. But your father—"

Here, Robert flinched slightly. It was true that in those first years, his mother had desperately told him he wasn't to blame for what had happened that day.

They'd never, however, discussed his father.

"Robert, I loved your father very, very much. But he was weak in some ways."

Shock had him lifting his stormy eyes to his mother's.

The duke had been formidable to say the least.

Something of what he was feeling must have showed on his face.

"Oh, he was powerful and brilliant, just like his son." She smiled before sobering. "But he was weak in ways that truly mattered. He insisted that life go back to normal, for your sake, and I saw the merit in that. But he never tried to really heal from Gina's death. Normal to him meant things appearing to be fine, without them actually *being* fine. I didn't realise that back then. I just went along with it. Had he been more honest, more open about his grief, he would not have turned to alcohol and come to rely on it so greatly."

"But, Gina's death was because—"

"Tell me, Robert, do you drown your many sorrows in two bottles of brandy every single night?"

He had done, often. But not every single night. He didn't rely on it. Didn't need it.

"No," he admitted gruffly.

"You, who were a child when the accident occurred. You, who was there and tried to save her. You, who had the mantle of duke, the duchy, and all of its many responsibilities thrust onto your young and grieving shoulders?"

"No," he said again.

"Your father chose his path, Robert. He died because of his choices. *His* choices. And only his."

Robert said nothing as he allowed his mother's words to sink in.

She really didn't blame him for losing her husband only a few short years after losing her daughter?

"There is blame to share, for so many things. None of us are blameless for the events after Gina's death." His mother finished her drink, placed the glass on the floor, then stood and shook out her skirts.

"Loving you has gotten me out of bed every day. Being your mother has been my purpose in life. I failed you then, but I will not do so again. You *must* find a way to forgive yourself for what happened, or it will consume you. It's been slowly consuming you for years."

Robert remained in his seat, refusing to make eye contact with his mother.

Perhaps there was truth in what she said of his father. But not Gina.

"You have a wonderful heart, even encased as it currently is in ice. But please, my dear, please let someone in. You deserve to be happy. You deserve to share your soul."

Without another word, his mother left the room.

Their talk had been more honest and open than any they'd ever had, and it left him feeling raw and drained.

But more than that, it had chipped away a tiny piece of his armour.

And that was no good.

For who would ever want to share a soul as black as his?

Chapter Nine

THE MASTER WAS in a towering rage.

That's what Bessie had whispered that morning as she'd brought Abigail her chocolate and helped her into a simple morning gown.

Riding was off the table for a while, until she could do so without remembering every minute detail of her kiss with Robert Forsythe.

When she'd seen him at breakfast the morning after he'd insulted her so, he'd offered a stilted apology, which she'd awkwardly accepted.

And then they'd both sat in silence, whilst the dowager smoothly made conversation between them with all the grace of, well, a duchess.

God help the woman who married the current duke.

Keeping him from scaring the wits out of or scaring off every person in the vicinity would be a monstrous task.

When she'd asked Bessie what exactly had set him up in the boughs this morning, she'd been informed non-too-sweetly that it was the flowers Abigail kept parading around the house.

It was ridiculous in the extreme that the man should have such an aversion to harmless things like flowers.

But this wasn't her house, praise the Lord! And she had no desire to have him take his towering mood out on the poor staff who worked for him.

So, Abby had apologised profusely, promised to never bring another bloom into the house, and now here she stood outside his closed study door, shaking with trepidation and all manner of other emotions she didn't want to explore.

Just knock, she was telling herself firmly. *Lift your hand and knock.*

Um…no, came the answer from another part of her brain. Clearly, the more logical part that didn't actually have a death wish.

She had marched down here, nearly tripping over her pale blue skirts, determined to take the blame for the flowers and his subsequent temper. She would appeal to his possibly non-existent better nature, and ask that he be nicer to the staff who had fetched her the vases she'd requested that morning after an early stroll.

But as she stood here, her bravery seemed to be deserting her with every second that passed.

The study door might as well have been the gates to Hell, so scared did she feel.

Perhaps he should have *"Abandon Hope, All Ye Who Enter Here"* engraved on the woodwork.

She smiled to herself, distracted by her thoughts. She'd only read Dante's work last year and had been enthralled by it.

Did Robert Forsythe read Dante? Probably not, she conceded.

Though the subject matter of that particular book would suit his mood no end.

A sudden crash, followed by a loud and rather impressive string of expletives sounded from inside the room, and Abigail nearly jumped from her skin.

Perhaps it would be better to come back later…

"You know, if you stand there long enough, the door might just disappear."

Abby whipped around at the sound of James's voice, and her cheeks flamed with embarrassment at having been caught lurking outside the duke's study.

"Good morning, James." She smiled brightly, feigning nonchalance.

"Abby, what on earth are you doing?" he responded, grinning at her.

"I-I was just—well the maid said h-his grace was angry about the flowers, and since it was my fault, I thought—"

"You thought," James smoothly interrupted her, "that you'd go charging in defending everyone's honour. And now you're scared because—well, it's

Robert."

"I am not scared," she defended hotly. Which was a lie. But still.

James merely raised a brow in response, and it was enough to set her to banging on the door before she even thought it through.

There was an immediate cessation in the swearing before the duke's deep baritone commanded that she enter.

"Good luck," James whispered with a grin, and her answering rude gesture sent him off down the corridor chuckling as he went.

Abigail opened the door and stepped inside the room, feeling as though she were walking to the gallows.

Honestly, this man was the most terrifying, hand-some, brooding, strong, powerful—

"Miss Langton?"

"Yes? What?"

She looked up to see the duke frowning down at her.

"I asked if I might help you, since you've come to my study."

Once again, heat flooded her cheeks. She'd been wantonly ogling the man while he stood there awaiting her answer.

He towered above her, and the severity of his black jacket only made his eyes seem more silver, more striking.

The fawn breeches that encased his legs couldn't hide the muscles there, and his—

"Miss Langton?"

"Oh dear," she blurted in response.

Abigail Langton. Stop it right now, she scolded herself.

Lord Montvale was staring at her as though she'd run mad, which seemed fair given the situation.

But it was slightly embarrassing nonetheless.

"Miss Langton, I am a busy man. So if there's nothing that you want?"

This wasn't going at all as she'd planned and her embarrassment, coupled with all sorts of memories of his kiss, and his lifting her onto her horse, and his being so rude to her and mean to the servants loosened her tongue.

"I want you to stop being so mean to everyone," she blurted.

A deafening silence met her outburst.

After an age, he spoke so softly that immediately Abigail was on her guard.

"I beg your pardon?" he whispered.

"Well, it's just that y-you haven't been happy with the flowers, I understand. A-and the servants, well they aren't to blame," she muttered.

Had a hole ever opened in the ground and swallowed someone, just because they wished it so?

Probably not, but oh would now be an excellent time for such an event to occur.

"I'm well aware of who has been covering my home in flowers, Miss Langton," he said softly, dangerously.

"Oh. Well, yes. So—"

"What I am less clear on," he continued, prowling—yes, prowling—closer to her.

Abigail felt herself back away on instinct.

"Is why my home continues to be flooded with flowers after I expressly said that I do not care for them."

"R-right," she croaked, as he took another step forward and she stepped back.

"Care to explain?"

She came to an abrupt halt as her back came into sudden contact with the wall.

Robert stopped mere inches from her.

Abby sighed, knowing that she was about to sound utterly ridiculous to a man who saw sentimentality as a weakness.

"My parents," she began, still unable to take a proper breath with him so deliciously close to her. "They didn't—well, I was—" She drew to a stop, wondering how she could possibly put into words how unwanted she'd been.

"Let's just say that I was more an inconvenience than a beloved firstborn." She tried to smile but suspected the expression was more grimace than ought else.

"Anyway, once, when I was eight and my sisters were six and four, we caught a fever. We were sick and bedridden for weeks. The doctor came every day and just seemed to make it worse." She grinned. "Ally and Beth got better and were able to leave the nursery, but I was sick for weeks longer and stuck inside, miserable and alone for hours at a time."

Abigail couldn't meet Robert's eyes as she spoke, staring furiously at his cravat instead.

She had no doubt that he would be bored stiff by her sad little tale. And it certainly wouldn't sway him, she knew. He was unswayable.

Still, she'd started now, so she might as well plough on.

"One day, I was alone as usual, lying in bed and feeling mightily sorry for myself, when my mother came in. She'd checked on us occasionally but for the most part, our care had been left firmly in the hands of our nurse and governess."

Abby swallowed a sudden, unexpected lump in her throat.

"I was so pleased to see her. Even my mother's company was better than none at all," she grinned.

"She came in and she was carrying a bouquet of wildflowers. She had been for a walk, she said, and spotted them in a field near our house. And she knew that I was lonely and sad, so she picked them. My mother, who never got her hands dirty, who never did anything for herself if she could help it, got down on her knees and picked me some wildflowers, just to cheer me up. It never happened again. A visit alone, I mean."

Abigail blinked furiously as tears threatened. Tears would no doubt make him as uncomfortable as this conversation surely did.

"She never did anything for just me before then, or after. That one small thing—well, it meant the world to eight-year-old me. And ever since, I've picked wild-flowers."

Abigail drew to an embarrassed stop. She hadn't really meant to reveal so much of herself, and she felt exposed and vulnerable.

She heaved a sigh and finally brought herself to meet his gaze, feeling their impact immediately and fiercely.

"I just thought you'd get used to it," she finished, pitifully.

Abigail could hear the breathless quality to her voice but could do nothing to control it.

Standing so close to him, she was once again over-whelmed by the sheer size of him. The broadness of his shoulders. The masculinity that seemed to ooze from him.

His eyes were molten silver, surrounded by the thickest, darkest lashes she'd ever seen.

And he smelled divine; sandalwood, and brandy,

and pure, sinful temptation.

All of which was very pleasant, but hardly conducive to having one's thoughts in order.

He watched her for what seemed like an age, before finally laughing, a raw, husky sound that skittered along her nerves and set her heart pounding.

"I don't think I'll ever get used to this," he answered roughly.

Abby swallowed loudly past the sudden lump in her throat.

"You really don't like the flowers?" she whispered, her voice made crackly by the desire slamming into her. Maybe she had managed to sway him somewhat.

"I really don't like the flowers," he answered, leaning slightly closer.

So she hadn't swayed him at all, then. But she couldn't feel overly disappointed. Not when he was awakening so many other feelings within her.

If he wasn't careful, she'd end up in a puddle at his feet. And he probably wouldn't like that, either.

"W-well, I'm sorry, then. But it's my fault, not the servants'."

"Oh, I know that," he answered dryly.

There was a pause fraught with tension.

"I-I should go then. And take care of them," Abby said, though she was loathe to move and very likely incapable of doing so.

"Yes, you should," he agreed, still watching her intently. Still agonisingly, wonderfully, torturously close.

"It seems a shame, though," she said, now feeling suddenly emboldened and a little mischievous. "They really are beautiful."

"Very beautiful," he agreed smoothly, still gazing at her, and all the air left her body with just those two words.

She knew he was going to kiss her even before his head dipped toward hers, before his hand lifted to cup her face, bringing her mouth up to meet his own.

And she craved it more than she craved oxygen to breathe.

She should probably push him away. Even slap him for good measure.

Instead, she lifted her hands to grip the front of his superfine as her knees gave out beneath her.

I need to stop this, she thought.

I need to leave.

But as he coaxed her lips open to plunge inside them, only one thought remained.

I need to keep kissing him.

I NEED TO stop kissing her.

Robert knew he should stop, yet nothing could have made him do so.

Not when he felt her hands grip the front of his

jacket. Not when he heard her sigh of capitulation. Certainly not when her tongue moved to dance with his own.

What was this madness she awoke within him? What spell did she cast upon him that made him forget everyone and everything but her and the feel of her in his arms?

She'd come in here looking for all the world like an innocent angel, blond and blue-eyed and bedecked in a gown that matched her eyes.

When the hell had he started noticing such things as the colour of women's fashions?

He'd been in high dudgeon all morning, he knew.

And now, only minutes later, he was terrifyingly close to losing all control and just drowning in this wave of passion that was consuming him.

Her and her damned flowers!

God, he'd give her every single bloom in Christendom if he could just continue holding her like this.

You deserve someone to share your soul.

Sudden and unbidden, his mother's words slammed into him with enough force to send him stumbling back.

Abby's wide blue eyes, glazed by what he assumed was a desire that matched his own, stared at him in confusion.

And who could blame her? He was acting like a madman. Cornering and kissing her in one moment, dragging himself away the next.

He was confusing himself, let alone her.

They stared at each other across the small distance he'd put between them, her breathing as laboured as his own.

He should apologise, of course. But he was not sorry.

Yet he should be. He could offer her nothing. Would not want to.

The silence went on, but he had no damned clue how to end it. And all the while, he had to clench his fists to stop from reaching for her.

"P-perhaps I should go?"

She phrased it like a question.

Was she waiting for him to ask her not to leave? Didn't she know the danger she was in, allowing herself to be kissed by a monster such as he?

She was too trusting, too innocent, too naïve. And she would be his undoing.

The thought was terrifying.

"Yes, you should," he growled, panic making his voice harsher than he intended.

He saw the surprise, the hurt, and it twisted his gut. But it was for the best.

Until he got control of this incessant *need* for her, she would do well to keep her distance.

Without another word, she turned and fled, and it was all he could do not to reach out and stop her.

Chapter Ten

THE MEETING WITH Lord Montvale this morning had not necessarily gone as Abby had planned.

A gross understatement, but she refused to think on it anymore.

She had, once again, hidden herself away for the remainder of the day.

The dowager didn't get many callers. Or any, really, she had told Abigail, since people were unilaterally terrified of her son.

But she called on several families regularly.

Abigail had cried off accompanying the older woman, citing a need to write to her mama.

This was a lie about which she felt slightly guilty, but she really wasn't up for company of any description, and she certainly didn't want the dowager watching her too closely for fear she would read the truth of what Abigail had been up to with her son.

Her guilt was assuaged slightly when she heard that James was being dragged along. Against his will but still, he was going. And a marquess was surely a far better addition to afternoon At Homes than an

American nobody.

Having spent the day almost exclusively in her room, Abby was now preparing herself to come face to face with the duke again at dinner.

Bessie had taken her white silk evening gown to be pressed while Abby had soaked in a lavender scented bath, and now the young maid was putting the finishing touches to an elaborate hairstyle that Abigail had no interest in.

"There we are, pretty as a picture, miss." Bessie smiled at Abigail's reflection, and she managed a small one back.

"You'd best get a move on, miss, or you'll be late to dinner. His grace won't be pleased."

At the mention of Lord Montvale, Abby's heart fluttered wildly.

"Is he a very unkind master, Bessie?" she asked.

Really, she shouldn't be questioning the staff, but she was desperate for any information about the brooding duke. And she knew that Bessie would have all sorts of information from the other maids.

Abigail had heard and seen his temper. She knew he could be surly and gruff.

Yet he listened to his mother's excited chatter with equanimity. He was doing all in his considerable power to ensure that their trip to London and subsequent stay would be as comfortable as possible, even though he really didn't want to go.

And when he held her and kissed her, he was so gentle, even though she could feel the strength of the passion he held in check, lurking beneath the surface.

And shocking though it was, she wanted to be the one to make that control snap, to experience the full force of his desire.

"Unkind, miss?"

Bessie's voice snapped Abigail from her highly inappropriate musings. The man was turning her into a veritable hussy!

"No, he's not unkind. Nobody has ever seen him in a good mood," the girl continued frankly. "But none have ever experienced unkindness at his hands. He's a fair and generous boss. Takes very good care of his tenants and servants, so say the maids."

Abigail tried to ignore the feeling of relief that swept over her. It was really nothing to do with her, how he treated his staff. Yet she couldn't help but be pleased that he treated them well.

"He's just so *grumpy*," Bessie continued, earning a smile from Abigail. "And you wouldn't want to cross him. Why, just this morning, young Milly was telling me quite the tale. Last year, he found out one of the footmen had—"

Bessie stopped abruptly, meeting Abigail's eyes in the mirror and flushing slightly.

"Do go on," Abigail urged.

"I shouldn't, miss," the maid mumbled, fussing

with Abby's curls. "It wouldn't be right to speak of such things to a gently bred lady."

Abby reached up to stop Bessie's bothering of her hair before turning on the vanity's bench so she could face the other girl.

She was quite sure that a gently-bred English lady of deportment would never grab hold of a maid so she could interrogate the servant about scandalous actions, but hang deportment! She needed to know.

"I won't tell a single soul that you divulged this information, Bessie," she promised, pulling the girl gently to sit beside her on the velvet bench.

"And, really, if Lord Montvale's behaviour is, is *dangerous...*" She whispered the word for dramatic effect but felt a crackle of guilt as she did so. He was a lot of things, but she'd never felt in any danger with him, and it felt wrong that she should make such accusations or implications.

Still, needs must.

And it worked, too.

Bessie's eyes widened, and she shook her brown curls at an alarming rate.

"Oh no, miss. You mustn't think that his grace did anything that would make him a danger to a young woman. Tis the exact opposite, in fact!"

Abby frowned in confusion, and Bessie blinked at her a couple of times before sighing in resignation.

"Very well, I'll tell you. But if Mrs. Johnson finds

out I've been telling you servants' gossip, she'll have my head."

Abby didn't blame Bessie for fearing the redoubtable housekeeper, but she assured Bessie that anything told to her in confidence would remain so and not leave the room.

"Well, miss, it's like this," Bessie finally began. "They'd a footman come up from London. He'd worked with a friend of his grace's. Not sure which one, not that he has many. Anyway, none of the girls liked him from the second he arrived. Always lurking in corners, creeping around where our bedchambers are."

Abby could see the revulsion in Bessie's eyes, and she reached out to pat the young girl's hand supportively.

"One of the girls, Lucy, was the sweetest little thing you could ever meet, Milly said. She wasn't very bright, Lord save her, but her da had died when she was a lass and her ma was too sick to work."

Abby's stomach clenched in apprehension of what she suspected was to come in the story.

"Freddie, that was the name of the scoundrel, well he took a liking to her and one night he convinced her to go for a walk round the stables with him."

Bessie snorted, and a flash of anger lit her brown eyes.

"A walk my ar—"

She glanced quickly at Abby, blushing slightly.

"Well, anyway, off they went and of course, when they were out of sight he—well, he—"

"Oh no, Bessie."

Abby was distraught, but the young maid was quick to reassure her.

"He tried, miss," she said sombrely. There was no need to speak the words. They both knew what the blackguard had done.

"But by the grace of God, Lord Montvale was out by the stables that night, and he heard poor Lucy's screams."

Abby's heart was hammering as she listened to Bessie's tale.

Her heart wrenched painfully at the thought of the poor, innocent girl who'd found herself in the clutches of such a man.

She knew how it was, in the usual way of things.

Females of the serving classes were often treated thus; raped, abused, then discarded by men from all walks of life.

It was beyond despicable, and she despised it.

"His grace ran to where they were. The commotion woke some of the stable hands, and they filled the house workers in on what happened."

The clock on the mantle chimed, interrupting Bessie's recounting of the event, and she glanced up at it before jumping from her seat.

"Gracious, miss, you'll be late to dinner. I shouldn't have been rabbiting on so, if—"

"Bessie." Abby's tone was sharper than she'd intended, and she smiled up at the younger girl to soften its effects. "I want to hear the rest of the story. If I am late to dinner, I shall take full responsibility. But for now, please do go on."

Bessie sighed in resignation.

"There's not much left to say, in any case," she said, moving to pick up Abby's satin evening gloves, smoothing them as she came back and began to help Abby's hands into them.

"By all accounts, his grace was furious. He beat the man to a pulp, the stable lads said. It took five of them to get him off the blighter, and even that was a struggle. Called for the magistrate but since he'd stopped any actual crime, Freddie walked free."

"The cad," Abby cried furiously.

"Right enough," Bessie agreed then her face split in a mischievous grin. "Course, he walked free with a permanent limp and not a penny in his pocket," she said. "And his grace warned him never to set foot in Northumberland again, which I'll warrant he won't, if he knows what's good for him. He's lucky he weren't killed. His grace also made sure to inform the blighter that he would be keeping tabs on him. And should he ever get wind that Freddie had put a hand on another young miss, his grace would see him hanged."

Abby could feel no sympathy for the man.

Her heart fluttered wildly at the knowledge of Robert's defence of poor, young Lucy, and she didn't care to examine what this tender feeling rising up in her was.

Robert would defend the honour of a servant girl without a moment's pause. And he was certainly big and strong enough to do so.

Imagine how he would protect a woman he cared about...

"Miss?"

Abby flushed slightly as she realised that her silly, romantic thoughts had wandered to the duke once more.

"What happened to Lucy, Bessie? Is she still here?"

"No, miss."

Abby stood and shook out her white satin skirts whilst Bessie fetched a dusky pink shawl that matched the piping on the gown.

"Milly said his grace enquired as to her circumstances and when he heard what hardships she and her ma had suffered, he set them up in a small cottage free of charge. Lucy helps the local seamstress, and his grace makes sure that her mother is well taken care of."

Abby's heart fluttered again.

It seemed Robert Forsythe was far more wonderful than he wanted people to know.

"I wonder then that he's called a monster," she said

boldly, knowing that Bessie would have heard such things, given she had already become firm friends with the local girls.

"Nobody outside of the estate workers know Lucy's story, miss," she said. "His grace forbade them to tell anyone, and much as we servants like to talk, ain't one of us brave enough to go against his wishes."

No, she probably wouldn't be either.

Yet she'd defied him over the flowers he so despised.

"But he is mightily bad-tempered, miss, at the best of times. And you could never accuse him of being friendly. Scares the wits out of the menfolk, that's for sure. It's just that we know he'd never hurt a woman."

That was true. Hadn't she, herself, already known instinctively that he wouldn't hurt her? And he'd been more than friendly when he'd taken her in his arms.

Abby felt the heat rise in her cheeks once more.

"Well, I should go," she said briskly, taking the proffered shawl. "Thank you for telling me, Bessie."

The young lady smiled in response.

Just as Abby was about to step through the door, the young maid spoke again.

"I don't think he's a monster, miss. But he sure does act like one at times."

"Will London really be so terrible?"

Robert raised a brow in response to James's frankly ridiculous question.

Yes, it would be so terrible.

He had absolutely no desire to be around other people at the best of times.

But in London? Where people gawped at him, whispered about him or worse—tried to befriend him—was beyond the pale.

And that wasn't even the worst part. No, the worst part was the desperate debutantes and their drill sergeant mothers, who even though they feared him, would still make ever more desperate attempts to bring him up to scratch. Fear, after all, was no match for wealth and a title.

The fact of the matter was that it was unsafe to be a single, wealthy, titled man in London during the Season.

And a duke was in more danger than most.

He couldn't think of a single thing worse than having to fend off silly young women.

The door to the drawing room opened wider than it had been, and Abigail Langton swept into the room, smiling as his mother moved to greet her.

Robert's breath caught in his throat as he studied the young lady that was turning his world upside down.

The dowager pulled her toward the couple she'd

been conversing with, the local magistrate and his wife.

There were few people Robert tolerated as guests in Montvale Hall. The magistrate was a bit too jolly for his liking, but his mother enjoyed the company of the rotund man's wife, and so they were invited to dine. Occasionally, but it was enough to keep his mother happy.

Miss Abigail Langton.

How could one, tiny termagant cause such chaos within him?

He watched as she moved across the room, her white satin gown swishing around her ankles as she went.

She looked like the very embodiment of an angel; all blond curls, wide blue eyes, and virginal white skirts.

The dress encased her in a way that was everything proper but all the more tempting for it, and he felt a sudden, visceral desperation to strip it from her and see what lay beneath.

Which he shouldn't be feeling, of course.

They were a study in opposites, she and he.

Abby walked into a room and lit it up with her radiant smile.

He walked into a room, and people scurried to the corners as fast as they could travel.

She was resplendent in white and pink and lightness.

He wore all black as was his custom, only the white of his shirt and cravat offering any sort of relief from the darkness of his attire.

And she was smiling. A real, genuine smile that made her eyes sparkle and appear as pools of the clearest waters.

If he ever properly smiled, he was quite sure his face would crack.

It must be true, then, that opposites attract.

Because he'd never been more attracted to anyone in his life.

"Now you see why I need you in London." James, having been completely forgotten by Robert, spoke quietly by his side. "I'll be fighting them off in droves."

Robert's stomach roiled as James's words sank in, and an ugly jealousy crawled through his veins.

He had thought that fighting off young ladies was the worst thing about this proposed trip to London?

How laughable.

The worst thing would be watching Abigail Langton pick some ridiculous dandy or other to marry and walking out of his life forever.

Chapter Eleven

A BIGAIL WINCED SLIGHTLY at the magistrate's wife's loud braying.

She was a lovely woman, but good Lord was she loud.

Still, the dowager had whispered to her, she could use the occasion to practice equanimity in the face of annoying behaviour.

A skill that was apparently absolutely necessary if one were to survive a Season among the *haute monde*.

The butler had rung the bell, and their small party was making their way to the dining room.

The magistrate, a Mr. Carlson, was escorting Abby, his chitchat a welcome distraction from her riotous emotions.

As soon as she'd walked into the drawing room an hour ago, she'd been aware of Lord Montvale glowering at her from the corner.

This *something* she felt around him was growing stronger by the day, and it was all she could do to stop herself from going over there and throwing herself in his arms.

Not the behaviour, she supposed, of a proper young lady on the cusp of her first Season.

Ironically enough, she felt her excitement for the upcoming trip to Town waning by the day.

It had all seemed so romantic to Abby back in New York; sail off to pastures new, meet a dashing English lord, and fall in love with him. Marry and have babies and live in the rolling English countryside for the rest of her days.

She would visit and write her family, naturally. But the truth was though she was close to her sisters, Abigail's parents had never been overtly loving or nurturing.

She wasn't sure they'd grieve the emigration of their eldest daughter. In fact, she was quite sure they wouldn't.

It had all seemed so wonderful.

And it was.

She loved it here. But that was the problem. She loved it *here*. But she wouldn't be *here*.

If she were to marry someone this Season, Lord only knew where she'd end up.

Not at Montvale Hall. Not near the crashing, un-forgiving ocean, or the rugged beauty of the cliffs.

Not in the village where the locals knew and chat-ted to her as though she were one of them.

And not, Abby swallowed past a sudden lump in her throat, with *him*.

Upon entering the dining room, Abby noticed with some dismay that the table was bedecked with multiple vases of the wildflowers she'd picked.

Oh dear.

Mrs Carlson exclaimed over the loveliness of the arrangements, and Abby found herself wincing again.

She dared a look at the formidable duke and startled when she found him staring at her, his molten silver eyes boring into her and causing her insides to flip-flop in an alarming fashion.

She was going to be in trouble. Again.

Before she had known flowers were such a colossal problem for the master of the house, Abby had asked the butler to ensure the table be filled with them for the dowager's guests. She wanted the older lady to enjoy her evening since she had confessed to Abby that she didn't get to entertain very often.

But with everything that had happened since, namely being kissed senseless by the man currently shooting daggers at her, she'd forgotten to tell the butler that the flowers were a very unwelcome addition to the evening's festivities.

However, it seemed the servant hadn't needed Abby to tell him, for at that moment, he hurried into the room. Hurried, not glided.

"Forgive me, your grace," he said as smoothly as ever, but his eyes darted to Abigail's before they moved back to Lord Montvale. "It will be but a moment to remove the vases."

While the rest of the party had moved to sit, the magistrate was still holding Abby's chair for her, but his wife's voice was echoing so loudly, he thankfully couldn't hear this exchange.

The butler raised a hand, and a small army of footmen came forward to remove the offending items.

Never had she known such a fuss about a few flowers, for heaven's sake!

Before any of them touched a vase, however, Robert spoke.

"Leave them," he said.

Abby's eyes darted to his, and she saw that he was still gazing at her.

Her heart hammered against her chest.

"Really?" she blurted, before she could help herself. Nor could she contain her grin.

It could have been her imagination, of course, but she thought she detected a tiny, fleeting smile in response.

"Really," he answered, his eyes never leaving hers. "I'm getting used to them."

HE WAS GOING soft in the head.

There was no other explanation.

Why else would he have left his table covered in her

flowers?

Why else would he have felt like puffing out his chest in pride when Abigail had smiled at him?

Why else would he have had to fight so hard to keep from smiling back at her?

And why did that smile in response to his small gesture make him want to get her the moon and stars from the sky, if only to have her look at him like that again?

Ridiculous.

He leaned against the balustrade of the veranda that surrounded the living floors of the house.

Their dinner party had, thankfully, ended some hours ago, and after a snifter or two of brandy with James, his friend had bade him goodnight.

And now Robert stood here alone, the bright moonlight illuminating the gardens below him.

The last few days had been hard for Robert.

He'd locked away all traces of emotion many moons ago, yet within these weeks he'd had an actual, real conversation with his mother.

One which hadn't destroyed him, as he'd feared. If anything, it had healed something inside him.

It wasn't enough to appease his guilt; that would forever remain a shackle around his heart.

But it had bridged a chasm he hadn't even known was between him and his mother, and he began to think perhaps it was true that she didn't blame him.

Didn't hate him.

And then, of course, there was his incessant man-handling of the young woman who was staying under his roof, and who should have been safe from such things.

Why couldn't he keep his hands off her? Why didn't he want to?

Robert didn't dally with innocents. Certainly not innocents who were related to his best friend.

But damn it, he had no control around her.

He, who never lost control of anything.

Worse, she didn't seem to mind his manhandling. Seemed to take as much pleasure from it as he.

If this kept up, he'd begin to think he wasn't the monster that he'd always believed himself to be.

And that just wouldn't do.

He couldn't start believing himself capable of caring, truly caring about someone.

He couldn't believe himself capable of doing something stupid like allowing his home to be filled with flowers just because he knew it pleased a woman who was here to marry someone else.

In just two weeks, they'd arrive in London, and within two weeks of *that* he was quite sure she'd have proposals of marriage coming out her ears.

And she should marry, he knew. It was absolutely right that she should go there and marry someone and move far away from here, and from Robert.

Abigail Langton was made for marriage. She had a heart of gold. It was evidenced in the way she interacted with the servants, in the friendship that she'd struck up with his mother, in the wistfulness of her tone when she spoke of the sisters she'd left behind. In the story of her mother and the wildflowers that had touched Robert's heart in a way he would never have thought possible.

She was destined for a life filled with wildflowers, laughter, music, love, and babies with a man who could be trusted to keep them safe.

And Robert was not that man.

A movement in the garden below caught his eye, and his mouth went suddenly dry when he realised it was her.

As though he'd conjured her with his thoughts, Abigail came into view, strolling slowly between the rose bushes of the carefully designed garden below him.

He watched her pause here and there to run her fingers along a rose petal, or bend to inhale the fragrance of a bloom before moving on.

She wasn't dressed in her formal gown of earlier, but neither was she in night attire. He probably would have died on the spot if that had been the case.

As it was, he was finding it difficult to draw a breath from just seeing her glorious hair unpinned and cascading down her back in a riot of golden curls.

The moonlight made her seem ethereal, as though she weren't even really there. A sprite, too beautiful to be real.

And despite what he'd told himself just moments ago, Robert found his feet moving toward the steps that would lead him down into the garden and toward her.

IF SHE FAILED to fall asleep every time she thought of Robert Forsythe, she'd never sleep again.

Abigail had tossed and turned for hours before finally giving sleep up as a lost cause.

She didn't expect to run into anyone out in the garden at two in the morning, but even she with her crass American ways knew it wasn't at all proper to stroll about in a night rail, so she'd donned a simple white muslin that she could fasten up herself, foregoing the stays and undergarments that required help, and made her way to the gardens.

Perhaps a quick walk in the cool moonlight would tire her out.

She'd tried reading, but the hero of the novel she was trying to concentrate on reminded her far too much of the duke, and so she'd tossed the book aside in frustration.

Silly that she should read so much into the simple

gesture of him not removing flowers from the table. Yet that one gesture had made it impossible for her to think of anything but him.

Abigail had an awful suspicion that she was getting dangerously close to falling in—

"Couldn't sleep, hmm?"

With a squeal of fright, Abigail whipped around at the sound of a gruff, male voice behind her, and only Robert's arms darting out to catch her as she stumbled backwards saved her from landing on her backside in front of him. Again.

"Y-your grace," she managed breathlessly. "You scared me."

His mouth twisted in a sardonic semblance of a smile.

"Yes, I tend to have that effect on people."

She felt a wave of sympathy at his wry statement, though she was quite sure he would loathe her pity.

"I'm not afraid of you," she answered softly. "You just move very quietly for such a big man."

"I do?" he raised a brow, and it was all she could do to stop from reaching up and smoothing her finger along it.

For goodness sake! This would not do.

"You do," she said, dragging her mind back from all manner of inappropriate places. "Like a panther."

"And what do you know of panthers?"

She couldn't read his mood. If she were to guess,

she'd say it was playful, which was clearly madness. He wasn't the type to be playful.

Yet, he seemed brighter these last couple of days. Like the invisible burden that always weighed him down had lightened, if only a small amount.

"I know that they are stealthy," she answered with a smile. "And sneak up on you when you least expect it. You need your wits about you around them."

He pretended to consider her words, and Abby felt herself delighting in this side of him.

Which was terrible, of course. She didn't need this man endearing himself to her.

"True," he said with mock gravity. "But only if you're the type of prey a panther would be interested in."

It took a moment for the meaning of his words to sink in, and when it did, Abby felt her cheeks burn with humiliation.

Well, he couldn't have made his lack of interest in her any more obvious. And here she was, daydreaming about falling in love with the brute.

"Well, y-yes, of course." She tried to laugh, but it came out as a sort of maniacal twitter, which did nothing to improve her mood. "I'll bid you goodnight then, your grace."

A hand shot out and clasped her arm before she had time to move away.

"I am not the animal expert you clearly are, Miss

Langton." He spoke so smoothly, his tone sending shivers along her spine. And good heavens! Was that a *smile*? It was breath-taking! He appeared years younger and more handsome than any man had a right to be. "But one thing I know is you are the exact type of prey a panther such as I would devour."

Well, that did it. Without warning, Abby's heart took flight and landed very firmly in love with the man who stood holding her arm and stealing her breath.

"Which means," he continued softly. "That you're in danger."

"I'm still not frightened," she managed, even as her body felt as though it were catching fire.

He smiled again, and Abby felt that she could very much get used to seeing that expression on his face.

"That makes one of us," he whispered.

And then his lips were on her own, sending her up in flames once again.

Chapter Twelve

"REALLY, MY DEAR it wasn't that bad."

Abigail grimaced at the dowager who looked serenely back, though the tightness around her lips gave her away.

"Not that bad?" Abigail exclaimed. "It was awful. *I* was awful."

"Lady Hester has been wearing those unfashionable gowns for years, Abigail, with those hideous hoops. You might very well have helped her in the long run."

Abby raised a brow in the dowager's direction. It was terribly sweet of the older lady to try to make her feel better, but even in America where the rules weren't as stringent or numerous as here, Abigail's actions would have caused a scandal.

"Helped her by throwing her dog across the room?"

"*Accidentally* throwing him across the room," the dowager corrected. "It was he who loosened his teeth on your skirts. Odious little creature."

"Helped her by knocking her backwards off her chair?" Abigail asked.

"It's not your fault Hester's chairs can't withstand

sudden movement," the dowager replied stoutly. "And you stumbled into her. That wasn't on purpose."

"And—and showing her, her *undergarments* to the vicar?" Abby repeated, her cheeks scalding with remembered embarrassment.

"Er, yes. Well. That was rather unfortunate. But you weren't to know the vicar would arrive at that moment and, as I said, if she wasn't wearing such out of mode clothes in the first place, it wouldn't have happened. Those hooped skirts were the work of the devil."

"I think I'm finding all of this a little harder than I should," Abigail mumbled miserably. "And when we get to London and all those parties and gatherings. All those *people*, I'm just afraid I'll embarrass myself. That I'll embarrass you."

Unbidden, an image of Robert popped into her head.

Oh, Lord. She could only imagine what he would think of her less-than-graceful display in Lady Hester's drawing room.

Abigail had truly hoped that somehow her mother's natural grace and comportment would rub off on her eldest daughter.

Clearly, it hadn't.

And if she couldn't survive an afternoon of calls, how on earth would she survive a Season in London? A Season she didn't particularly want anymore.

Who could ever have imagined there were so many ways for a fifteen-minute visit to go so drastically wrong?

"My dear," the dowager interrupted Abigail's depressing musings, "This was one unfortunate call. That's all. We'll just—we'll just put it from our heads and forget it ever happened."

The dowager paused.

"And keep you away from dogs," she continued. "Just in case."

"You're sure it wasn't a disaster?" she asked Lady Montvale, desperate for reassurance.

"I'm sure," the dowager smiled, her tone mollifying.

It seemed sincere enough, and Abigail was able to breathe slightly easier.

Perhaps it wasn't so bad, after all.

"IT WAS DISASTROUS. Just disastrous, Robert. We simply don't have a choice."

Absolutely not."

"Darling, please be reasonable. This would be a wonderful opportunity for Miss Langton before we remove to Town."

Robert muttered a string of expletives that did nothing to lift his dark mood.

The last thing he wanted to think about was Abigail in Town with swains falling all over her, tempting her with their flowery words and ability to interact like a human being, and not a monster.

Since their kiss last night, Robert felt something had shifted inside him and for the first time in his life, he had no idea how to act around another person.

Usually, he found being rude and abrasive was enough to keep them at a distance, but more and more he found that he didn't want to keep Abigail at a distance. And he'd rather walk over hot coals than hurt her by being rude.

What the hell was happening to him?

"Mother." He spoke now with deliberate patience. "I have absolutely no intentions of hosting a party. You will have to find some other way to train Miss Langton to catch a husband."

"Catch a husband," his mother scoffed. "I'll be lucky to keep her name from the scandal sheets at this rate. The poor thing. It really wasn't her fault. But— well, practice can only do her good in this matter. I confess, during our hours together, I never felt the need to teach Miss Langton how not to fling animals at marchionesses, and tip people upside down."

Robert fought valiantly against the laughter threatening to explode from him.

He could imagine all too well the scenario his mother had described to him, her face lined with worry, her voice filled with remembered horror.

He had been pleased to hear that she'd reassured Abby on the way back to the Hall. He knew that the blonde beauty would be recriminating herself for her missteps.

Lady Hester was an old dragon and the worst sort of snob. She wouldn't have cared for Abby even if she'd behaved like one of the patronesses of Almack's. Abby was American, and that would have sealed her fate before she even entered the stuffy halls of Lady Hester's home.

"And I really do feel it is in Abigail's best interests to meet all of the people Lady Hester will have gotten to. Do some damage control. After all, a little scandal is fine. Welcomed even. It will get her talked about and sought after. But any true blemish on her reputation will be impossible to undo."

Robert's good humour vanished as quickly as it had come. His mother, he presumed, was talking about Abby having an unblemished reputation with which to catch a man to marry. And that was something he really didn't want to be a part of.

"All the more reason for me not to host a party. It will be bad enough having people come here to gawk at me. But if they get a whiff of scandal about Miss Langton, they'll come in their droves. And I don't want that at my house."

The dowager, however, wouldn't be silenced on the

matter.

Robert let her drone on, not really paying attention. He wondered if perhaps he should tell her that he'd been kissing her young protégée senseless at every possible opportunity.

Probably not.

But he was tempted to, if only to assure her that Abigail didn't need practice to be a success in Town.

All she would have to do is walk into a room and the *ton* were sure to be putty in her hands. And any man who was lucky enough to hold her in his arms would propose on the spot.

That was if Robert didn't tear the bastard apart limb from limb.

"Robert, are you even listening?"

No, he wasn't. He was working himself into a jealous temper because of an imaginary man putting his hands on Abigail.

It was official. He was only fit for Bedlam.

"We're leaving in two weeks, Mother. What use is it having a party now?"

His mother looked a little flustered, something Robert had never seen in his life, and it threw him slightly. What was she about?

"I just—I would like to give Miss Langton the opportunity to meet some acquaintances that we're sure to come across in Town and polish her social graces. It's very daunting, you know, knowing nobody. Surely you see the merit in easing the girl's way?"

It seemed as shoddy a reason as he'd ever heard, but Robert knew better than to try and understand the female psyche. Besides, his mother had said it would make things easier for Abigail. And damn him for his foolishness, but he found himself wanting to make life easier for her in any way he could.

It seemed to him as though his mother's smile of triumph was tinged with something else he couldn't quite put into words. She looked very much as though a plan was coming together.

But he didn't have time to worry about such things now.

He'd told James and Abigail that he'd join them on an afternoon ride and fool that he was, he wanted to spend time with her before they went to London and the hoards descended.

"I THINK I really must live near the sea." Abigail smiled happily at her companions as their mounts crested a hill and the formidable Montvale Hall came into view.

To think that only a short time ago she had found the house frightening and intimidating. Now the idea of leaving it forever was anathema to her.

Not unlike its owner.

But she couldn't allow herself to think such things

or she was liable to do something foolish, like cry or announce to Robert that she was madly in love with him, that she had no interest in London, and would much rather stay here forever with him.

"You'll have to take care to marry someone with a seat near the sea, then," James said.

Was it her imagination or did the silence following this statement seem strained?

Abigail risked a glance at the duke, but he was as stoic and impassive as ever.

"Perhaps I won't marry anyone," she quipped to lighten the suddenly tense atmosphere. "Perhaps I'll become a spinster and come live with you at Avondale, forcing you to do your familial duty, and cramping your bachelor lifestyle."

James made a theatrical face of mock horror, eliciting a laugh from her.

Montvale remained silent.

"The dowager wouldn't hear of it," James responded. "She's determined to marry you off. It's your fault we're having this silly party next week. If you hadn't tried to kill Lady Hester and her dog last week, we wouldn't be in this situation."

Abigail couldn't contain her groan.

She would be eternally grateful to the dowager for taking her under her wing as she had and helping her so much. In point of fact, the dowager had shown more maternal interest in Abigail than her own mother ever had. But the thought of what this party must be doing to Robert made her feel awful. She knew how he would despise such things.

"You aren't looking forward to the party?" Robert finally spoke, and Abby's eyes flew to his.

It was another cloudless, early spring day and in the sunlight, his eyes looked almost silver. But even as she watched, they changed to a wintry grey, darkened by some emotion she couldn't identify.

"I'm very grateful to your mother, and to you, for arranging it, and I'm acutely aware of the inconvenience of hosting at such short notice," she said carefully, not wanting to insult him. And then, because that mischievous streak of hers never seemed to go away, she continued on, "And of course, I am already such an inconvenience to you."

Her cheeky statement was met with a bark of laughter from James, and miracle of miracles, Robert's face lit with one of his elusive, earth-shattering smiles.

"You're an absolute hoyden, Miss Langton. Has anyone ever told you that?"

"Oh, frequently." She grinned, unrepentant.

And to her shock and pleasure, she earned herself an actual laugh.

It sounded hoarse, no doubt from lack of use. And both Robert and James looked as startled by it as she felt.

How far they'd come, that he would smile and even

laugh with her.

He was changing by the day.

It almost felt as though he were coming back to life.

And not just him. The Hall itself seemed to be coming alive, too. It was awakening like a spring dawn after a particularly bleak winter.

The servants were happier, the mood was lighter. Robert had even stopped complaining about the vases of wildflowers that Abigail now filled with abandon.

Foolishly, she couldn't help imaging what it would be like to live here with Robert, filling his house with flowers and his life with smiles.

Nothing could be better.

"Shall we return to the Hall, then?" James asked, mercifully oblivious to the wistful imaginings of his cousin. "I'm quite sure the dowager has all manner of tasks for the three of us."

All three of them sighed, each for his or her own reason.

"I suppose we must," Abby replied with a slight grimace. She simply hated being the one to cause any sort of discomfort to Robert.

"Well, you certainly must," James laughed. "As I said, it's your fault."

"I am aware of that, James," Abby scowled. "All this effort. I'm quite sure I'm not worth it."

"You're worth it."

Robert's softly spoken words reached her and

caused her heart to thud painfully.

She glanced up and locked eyes with his molten silver.

She forgot that James was present. Forgot everything in the face of his scrutiny.

What she wouldn't give to lean over and press her lips against his own.

In fact, without conscious thought, she felt her body move to do just that.

The sudden sound of James's coughing brought reality crashing back, and she blinked to break Robert's sinful spell.

Glancing at her cousin, who was now watching them both shrewdly, Abigail felt her cheeks heat.

"If you'll excuse me, I really must find the dowager."

Knowing how odd her behaviour was, and how senseless she must currently seem, Abigail kicked Lancelot into a canter and rode away from James's speculation and Robert's irresistibility.

THE SILENCE THAT Abigail left in her wake was deafening.

Robert resisted the urge to pull at his cravat. Or to run off after her.

He could have kicked himself for his stupidity.

No way would James let Robert get away with such a statement. And nor should he.

There would be questions, of that Robert was sure. But how to answer them?

James felt as protective of Abby as a big brother would. And he'd brought her here so the duchess could help her. Not, Robert assumed, for him to paw at her and say such intimate things.

Steeling himself for what would no doubt be an inquisition of epic proportions, Robert turned to face James.

But instead of looking furious, his oldest friend mere gazed placidly back at him.

And that made Robert feel decidedly wrong-footed, which he really didn't like.

"James, I—"

"Let's get back then," James said jovially. "Lest your mother send out a search party."

"That's it?" Robert blurted. "That's all you have to say?"

James studied him silently for what felt like eons.

Finally, he smiled an enigmatic smile that caused Robert to feel even more nervous.

"For now," James said with a grin before turning his mount and heading in the direction Abby just took.

Robert watched in shock as his friend rode away after the woman who had turned his world upside down.

Why wasn't James more upset?

If he knew even half of what Robert thought when Abby was around, or how many times he'd kissed her, Robert would have more than one bullet in him, he was certain.

Chapter Thirteen

THE EVENING WAS as tedious as Robert had known it would be. And it had only just begun.

He stood in the receiving line beside his mother, scowling at the never-ending queue of arriving guests.

It seemed that he'd created quite the stir when he'd sent out invitations to a ball at Montvale Hall.

Not least because an invitation to a ball hadn't been issued in eight years. While his father believed in keeping up appearances, Robert did not. As soon as he'd ascended to the title, Robert stopped hosting parties, and dinners, and anything else that meant having to spend time in the company of his peers.

Robert stood there, his mood growing steadily darker as more and more people came to gawp at him. He felt like a spectacle in a travelling circus.

"Smile, dear. You're scaring our guests," his mother whispered furiously, even as she maintained her smile for the stream of gentry coming through the doors.

"They can't be that scared, or they wouldn't be here," Robert bit back mutinously.

He noticed with grim satisfaction that most of the

arriving guests didn't quite meet his eye as they bowed and curtsied to him.

They were obviously nervous around him. No doubt terrified to be in the presence of the Monster of Montvale Hall.

The moniker bothered him more now than it ever had.

He was starting to think that perhaps he wasn't quite the monster he had assumed himself to be for all these years.

In these last weeks, he'd felt lighter. Younger.

Since his talk with his mother…

No, it wasn't just that. It was Abigail. Since she'd barrelled into his world and filled it with smiles and outrageousness, nonsensical talk about birds kissing, and an abundance of wildflowers, he felt something akin to happiness.

And more than that, he started to believe that he didn't have to carry the weight of his guilt and grief around forever. Certainly, he didn't have to let it consume his whole life.

Perhaps it was time to start focusing on something else. Something more positive. Something that could maybe make his soul worth sharing.

As if his thoughts had somehow made her appear, Robert looked up, and there she was.

Abby was making her way toward Robert and the dowager, oblivious to the commotion she was causing as she sailed through the crowd.

With her arm in James's, she glided toward him, not hearing the twittering from the ladies or noticing, Robert's temper flared, the lascivious glances from the gentlemen.

More than once he'd thought of her as doll-like with her golden curls and big blue eyes. Her skin as smooth as the finest china.

But tonight, she looked all real, all woman.

Her dress was a deep, peacock blue. Either his mother had failed to inform Abigail of the traditions regarding single ladies being confined to pastels or whites, or Abby had chosen to flout the nonsensical rule.

Whatever the reason, Robert was eternally grateful.

For the dress, the colour brightening the blue of her eyes, the cut skimming her body like a lover's caress, merely confirmed what he already knew—she was the most beautiful thing he'd ever seen.

And he wanted her with a fierceness he'd never before felt.

James and Abby came to a stop in front of Robert and his mother, and even though James issued a greeting, Robert could not drag his eyes from Abigail.

She dipped a curtsy, first to his mother, then to him, blushing prettily when she caught his gaze.

"My dear, you look beautiful." The dowager leaned forward to kiss Abigail on the cheek. "I knew you would be an absolute sensation."

"A bold colour choice, I thought." James grinned. "I brought her here so you could school her in the ways of decorum, your grace, not be even more scandalous than when she arrived."

Because Robert was watching her so closely, he saw the delicate blush that came to her cheeks at James's joking words.

"Oh, fiddlesticks." The dowager waved off his concerns. "We are not in London yet, so the rules aren't quite as rigid. Besides, I wanted people talking about her before we arrived. And it's working," she finished triumphantly.

At the dowager's words, Abby's eyes widened then darted around the room.

The blush in her cheeks grew scarlet as she saw for the first time the effect she was having.

"Goodness," she laughed. "Are you sure this is a good idea, your grace?"

"It is a terrific idea" the dowager responded stoutly. "You're already beautiful, dear. There's no hiding that. When we get to Town, we'll make sure you're in more appropriate colours."

Abigail took a deep breath before pasting a determined smile on her face.

"You know best," she said. "Though—every other young lady seems to be in white. I look—"

"Perfect."

The word slipped out before he could retract it. But it was true, and Robert hated seeing her overset, though he refused to examine why.

"You look perfect," he repeated softly.

Though Robert could feel the stares of his mother and best friend boring into him, he kept his gaze trained only on Abigail.

She swallowed hard before smiling tentatively up at him.

"Thank you, your grace," she said quietly.

The heavy silence was finally broken by the dowager.

"Well, it's time to start the dancing. Robert, I know that you will not open the ball, but if James—"

"Miss Langton," Robert cut across his mother. "Would you do me the honour of dancing the first with me?"

He didn't know what had gotten into him.

He usually played his cards so close to his chest. Yet here he was, telling Abby that she looked perfect and asking her to dance the opening cotillion.

And he knew what this would mean. It would send tongues wagging like never before.

The gossip would spread like wildfire.

The monster and the American beauty.

He could just imagine what it would mean for Abby's entrée into Society.

Plus, it would practically wave a banner above his

head saying that he was ready to walk amongst the living again. And with that came ghastly invitations, afternoon colours and, God help him, matchmakers.

Robert wasn't ready for that.

He couldn't get a handle on how he felt about so many things in his life right now. He was nowhere near ready to be a subject of London chatter.

And yet…

The idea of anyone else being the one to take Abigail in his arms was enough to make him murderous.

So, he'd blurted out the request before the dowager could send her off to be mobbed by dandies and fops.

And now he knew he had set himself up for his mother's interrogation, James's suspicion, and Abigail's—

Delight?

He could swear that's what he was looking at in her face, in her cornflower eyes as they lit up.

"I'd be honoured, your grace." She smiled, and Robert could practically feel another brick crumbling from the wall around his heart.

Sparing not a glance for his mother or James, Robert held out his arm.

As soon as Abigail placed her white-gloved hand on his elbow, memories of their kisses flooded his senses.

His instinct was to recoil. Run away and drown in his darkness and his grief.

But he wouldn't do it. Not this night.

Tonight, he would dance with a beautiful woman, watch his mother blossom into a living, breathing person again, and maybe even have a small reprieve from the monster inside him.

ABIGAIL TRIED TO keep the smile on her face as Robert escorted her to the centre of the ballroom.

But it was becoming steadily more difficult.

She'd never considered herself to be the shy or retiring type, but the level of scrutiny she was currently under was excruciating.

It could be the daring colour the dowager had convinced her it would be all right to wear.

It could be that she was new to these shores and people were curious about her.

However, she suspected that it was more likely to be the fact that the Monster of Montvale Hall himself was not only hosting a ball in his home but was about to open it.

With a stranger.

In New York, such a thing would cause weeks' worth of gossip. In a Northumberland village, it would probably be talked about for years.

She heaved a sigh, trying to rally her courage.

People started to tentatively couple up on either

side of her and Robert, but they certainly kept their distance.

Abigail's heart hammered. Not just because of the blatant staring she was currently enduring but because in just moments, Robert would be touching her, dancing with her.

"That was quite a sigh, Abby. Are you regretting your agreement to dance with me?"

He spoke quietly enough for his words to reach her ears alone, and Abby blinked up at him, shocked and pleased to see a smile playing around his lips.

He was teasing her, she realised. Actually teasing. He didn't even look like he'd been forced into the room against his will.

In light of his nonchalance about the attention they were drawing, Abby's own courage grew, and she found herself suddenly not caring who was looking at them or why.

All that mattered was that Robert was holding her hand and smiling down at her and looking younger and more carefree than she'd ever seen him.

Abby arched a brow as the orchestra plucked out the opening chords of the dance.

"I'm not sure yet, your grace," she quipped. "I have never seen you dance. For all I know, you have two left feet, which you will tramp all over me."

Robert treated her to one of his swift, heart-stopping grins.

"Minx," he growled softly, sending all manner of delicious shivers along her spine. "I'll have you know, I am an impeccable dancer."

Abby laughed at his haughty tone, relishing this new side of him.

She couldn't imagine what had affected such a change in him. Oh, but she loved it.

"Because you are such a prolific dancer?"

"Oh, no. My dancing is so wonderful, I save it for very special occasions. To give the others a chance." He winked.

"And this is a special occasion?" she asked.

He bowed, and she curtsied as the beginning strains of the music began.

In seconds, any meaningful conversation would be rendered nigh on impossible.

"It is," he answered simply.

The dance began, and Robert took her hand, stepping toward her then back.

"What makes it so special?" she asked.

A sudden gleam of emotion turned his eyes to molten silver, and Abigail's heart fluttered wildly in response.

"You do," he whispered before turning away to continue the dance.

Chapter Fourteen

THE WIND PLAYED havoc with the candle Abby clutched in her hand as she tip-toed down the corridor of the dark, silent Hall.

One would have thought that so many hours of dancing would result in exhaustion, but no. Sleep had eluded her for hours, and she was no closer to dozing off than she had been when she'd first retired.

The ball had been a resounding success, and the dowager had been beside herself as she spoke of the sensation Abby had been.

Yet Abby had not cared about being a sensation. She hadn't cared that her dance card had been quickly filled.

The only dances she'd cared about where the ones in Robert's arms. The opening cotillion and then, even now her heartbeat picked up, the supper waltz.

Abby had known at the beginning of the dance that her heart had been in very real danger.

And just as she'd suspected, when Robert had placed a hand around her waist to waltz with her, she had fallen hard and fast into love with him.

It was folly. Abigail knew that.

Robert might be opening up more. Smiling more. Even leaving wildflowers in his line of vision.

But he was a long way from someone who would open his heart to her. And she still didn't even know why.

James had said that Robert's story was his own to tell.

Yet he'd never given any indication that he would tell her. And she couldn't very well ask him!

How could she love a man who was so closed off to her, to everything? Yet love him she did.

So, here she was in the middle of this gigantic house, all alone and trying to remember the way to the kitchen.

Perhaps a hot drink would send her off to sleep.

It was better than tossing and turning in any case.

Cupping a protective hand around the flickering candlelight, Abigail moved on once again…

Straight into a table.

Biting her lip to keep from crying out and waking the entire household, she hopped around, grasping her toe and cursing the table that had sprung up from nowhere.

The candlestick fell to the ground with a thump, and she was plunged into darkness.

Only the moonlight shining through gaps in the drawn curtains gave any sort of relief from the black.

It was no use. She was cold and grumpy, and all she had for her efforts was a sore foot.

Giving her plan up for a lost cause, Abby turned to make her way back to her rooms.

A sudden sound halted her in her tracks, and she listened closer.

Had that been a groan? Where had it come from?

There!

The groan sounded louder still, and the air squeezed from Abby's lungs.

Whatever or whomever was making such a noise was obviously in extreme pain, and it hurt her heart to hear it.

A sudden shout rent the air, and Abby jumped from her skin.

It was coming from behind the door just beside her.

These were the family quarters.

She had been put near the dowager when she'd arrived, and James had been put in a room closer to Robert's.

Another groan made Abigail's heart twist painfully.

The voice was male. And she didn't think it was James.

She should leave. Just turn around and leave.

She absolutely, positively could not enter a man's bedchamber in the middle of the night. Or at any time, really.

She knew this.

Walk away, Abby, she told herself sternly.

And then, he cried out. "Please, no."

It was the most desolate, bleak thing Abby had ever heard, and she couldn't bare it.

Without giving herself a chance to change her mind or garner a modicum of common sense, Abigail twisted the doorknob and pushed Robert's bedroom door open.

Her heart was hammering so loudly in her chest that she was sure it would wake Robert and everyone else in the house.

But no. The night remained silent and still, save for the harsh breathing and occasional whimper from Robert.

Abigail stepped inside the room and then froze at the sight before her.

The curtains in this room had been left open so the pale moonlight illuminated the space, giving Abigail a clear view of what was inside.

Her first thought was that it clearly wasn't a master bedroom, given that it was the same size as her own bedchamber.

Her second was that she needed to get out of there. Fast.

Robert had obviously been unsettled for quite a while, judging by how the coverlet was twisted around his body.

His naked body.

Abigail's throat dried, and she found herself frozen to the spot.

The covers lay around his stomach, and she gave a prayer of thanks for that, at least.

Somehow, she didn't think his waking up to find a woman in a dead faint at the foot of his bed would be a positive experience for any of them.

But his muscled torso and arms were in full view, and though she knew she was courting danger, Abigail couldn't help herself. She stepped closer, her eyes fixed on the man lying before her.

She knew she should be ashamed of herself. Abigail had never considered herself to be voyeuristic, and she had certainly never considered herself the type of woman who would sneak into a man's room to ogle him.

But she'd never seen anything so—so beautiful! It was an odd way to describe a man of such size and strength, such blatant masculinity. Yet it was true.

The sinewy muscle, the smooth jaw, the mussed hair. It was beauty in its rawest form.

Robert suddenly groaned again, and the sound forced Abby into action.

What on earth was she thinking?

She dragged her eyes from Robert and made to move toward the door.

But just then, he shouted, "Stop!" and Abby spun

round, thinking he was speaking to her.

No, he was still asleep. But Abby's relief was short lived.

In her haste to turn around, she'd trodden on her night rail and she stumbled forward, toward the bed.

This was going to end badly.

Abigail pitched headfirst toward where Robert lay oblivious.

Luckily, she managed to land on her knees so that her entire body didn't fall on top of him where he slept.

Unluckily, she ended up directly beside his face.

She hit the ground with a loud thump, and instinctively reached out to break her fall.

To Abby's utter mortification, Robert's eyes snapped open just as her hands landed on either side of his head, and her face stopped inches from his own.

She watched as myriad emotions flicked through his eyes.

There was the leftover horror from what was evidently a terrible nightmare, then shock, presumably because he didn't usually waken to an unwanted face inches from his own. Finally, a desire so potent that her knees turned to liquid. Which was unfortunate since they were supporting her.

The fraught silence was broken only by Robert's laboured breathing. Abigail had stopped breathing the second his eyes had opened.

Finally, when her nerves were stretched to their

breaking point, Abigail couldn't take it any longer.

"Robert, I—"

She didn't even get a chance to finish whatever she'd been going to say.

With a muffled oath, Robert reached out a hand and pulled her face toward his for a wild, passionate kiss.

ROBERT WONDERED BRIEFLY if he'd finally descended into complete madness.

He had been in the throes of an ever-worsening nightmare.

And he'd thought he'd woken up.

Yet clearly not.

His nightmare had become his deepest fantasy. For it truly felt like he was kissing Abigail Langton.

And this dream felt more real than even the nightmare of moments ago.

The Abby of his dream gasped, and Robert took the opportunity to delve his tongue inside her mouth, tasting her and driving himself mad with desire.

God, he never wanted to wake up.

With a groan, he reached down and plucked her up from her prone position beside him.

What had she been doing on the floor, in any case? That was a first in the many dreams he'd had about her. So too was the *realness* of this one.

He wrapped his arms around her and rolled so she was underneath him, lowering his head to place a trail of kisses along her jaw, as he'd been desperate to do for weeks.

Her moan of pleasure filled the room, causing an answering painful lust inside of him.

Robert opened his eyes to gaze down at her, and—

Wait.

He opened his eyes to gaze down at her…

He opened his eyes!

Robert's thundering heart stopped dead in his chest as reality came crashing down around him.

Dear God. This was *real.* It was no dream. He was kissing Abigail. In his bedchamber. On his bed.

Robert jumped from the bed, staggering to the window, putting some much-needed distance between him and the woman who'd been haunting his dreams for weeks and had now, somehow, become very, very real.

He struggled to catch his breath as his sleep-fogged mind tried to make sense of what was going on.

Abigail had by now scrambled to her feet and was standing on the other side of the bed, staring at him, her eyes impossibly big in the moonlight.

A good thing, too, that the bed was now between them, for if she'd been any closer, Robert couldn't guarantee he'd have the strength to keep from reaching for her once more.

"Abigail." Desire made his voice gruff. "I'm sorry. I didn't—"

"No, *I'm* sorry," she blurted, and even in the darkness, he could sense that her cheeks were flaming. "I shouldn't have come in b-but…"

She trailed off, and Robert felt a sudden dread.

"Why did you come in?" he bit out. He didn't mean to be so sharp. But Robert's ghosts were his own business. And the last person he wanted to see that side of him was the woman facing him, though he couldn't say why exactly.

"I heard s-something. You sounded—that is, there was m-moaning and a shout and—"

She paused in her stuttering, and Robert felt a wave of shame wash over him.

He hadn't shown vulnerability to anyone since his childhood, and it made him feel defensive and deuced uncomfortable to know that the woman he—

He shied away from that thought before it could fully form.

This situation was bizarre enough without adding to the tense emotions flying around the room.

What he needed was to get her out of her, because he was acutely aware that they were still in his private rooms, and acutely aware of what they'd been doing only moments ago.

And then there was the small matter of his being

completely naked.

His control could only last so long.

"My apologies for disturbing your evening, Miss Langton."

"Miss Langton?" She sounded shocked by his formality.

But she didn't know he was hanging on by a thread.

"Robert, you've just—that is we've just—"

"Abby."

He interrupted, and even he could hear the desperation in his tone. But if she was going to start rehashing what had just happened on that bed, no amount of furniture between them was going to stop him from picking up where they'd left off.

And the fact that he sensed she wanted to as much as he did wasn't helping his control in any way.

"Please, for the love of God, do not speak of what just transpired here."

"Why not?" she demanded, and he couldn't help but smile.

She was an utter tearaway. He knew of no other woman who would find herself in such a precarious situation and not run away crying, or swoon from shock or some such nonsense.

No, Abigail would argue with the devil himself if the mood took her.

Robert pinched the bridge of his nose, struggling to maintain his composure.

"Because," he bit out. "It's bad enough that we're in my bedroom in the middle of the night, with no one around but us."

He stepped away from the window, closer to her, though he knew damn well he shouldn't.

"It's bad enough that I feel like my entire body is going up in flames every time I touch you."

He stepped closer still, until it was only the bed between them.

"And if you don't leave now, I'm not sure I'll be able to keep my distance as I should."

That would surely scare her off.

Abigail gazed at him for what seemed like an eternity before she shocked him yet again as soon as she opened that bloody mouth of hers.

He watched as her chin tilted up in what he was coming to recognise as a mark of defiance.

"Why should you keep your distance?" she asked boldly, and that barely banked fire of lust roared to life inside him.

But he'd heard the slightest tremor in her voice, and it was enough to make him hang onto the last remnant of self-control.

"You don't know what you're asking, Abby," he told her softly. "You're an innocent. Pure."

He laughed but there was no humour in it.

"You don't want to be sullied by a monster like me."

"You're not a monster, Robert," she protested immediately, and he hated how much it affected him, hearing his name on her lips. Because it made it so much harder to send her away.

"Trust me, sweetheart. I am the closest thing to a monster you're ever likely to meet."

She opened her mouth, no doubt to protest. But he didn't give her the chance.

"You need to leave while I still have the strength to let you walk away from me."

He watched her watching him.

He prayed that she would leave. Hoped that she would stay.

Finally, without another word, she turned and fled the room.

And Robert tried to ignore the pang in his chest as he watched her go.

Chapter Fifteen

IT WAS HARD to believe they were leaving for London in a mere week.

Abigail tried to muster some enthusiasm for the idea as she bent to fill her basket with wildflowers.

They grew in abundance around the cliffs.

And there would be none in London.

"For goodness sake," she scolded herself out loud. "All you've ever wanted was to come to London."

And that was true.

In New York, all she'd dreamt of was coming to England and spending a Season in London.

The problem was that since she'd arrived, she'd gotten herself a new dream.

A completely unrealistic, unattainable one.

It had been two days since she'd, well, broken into Robert's bedroom and watched him sleep.

It sounded awful in the stark light of day. It *was* awful. Abigail never would have thought that she'd act in such a way.

It was mortifying.

And worse still, not only had she watched him,

then *kissed him*— on his bed no less, but he'd practically had to throw her out of his bedchamber because instead of running like a proper lady would do, she'd stood there and argued with him.

Even now, days later, her cheeks heated.

How could she have acted in such a way?

Her mother always warned her that she'd get herself into trouble with her irresponsible, irrepressible spirit, and she'd been right.

The truth was, Abby had to swallow a sudden lump of shame, that if Robert hadn't sent her away, she mightn't have stopped him from doing whatever it was he had been alluding to.

What did that make her? A hussy, that's what!

After she'd left Robert's room, she hadn't gotten a wink of sleep, obviously. How could she have? After what had happened?

And then she'd locked herself away for two days, claiming a headache, because there was no way she could face him.

If Abigail hadn't lost her heart to Robert before that night, it certainly had happened then.

And he'd awakened something in her that night.

She'd gone into that room because she'd been worried about him. Concerned about what she'd heard.

His desolation had been like a physical blow to her, making her heart ache, making her desperate to help.

But when he'd opened his eyes and looked at her

with such naked desire, something had stirred within her. Something dark, wicked, and sinful.

Even now, Abigail felt her blood heat at the memory of how his lips had captured hers, of how it had felt to be lying in his bed, the weight of his body pressed deliciously along her own.

"Abigail."

Abby screeched with fright as a voice sounded just behind her.

Spinning around with a hand pressed to her heart, her eyes widened in dismay.

James was standing, wincing with his hands at his ears, and beside him was Robert, looking more handsome than ever and causing her heart to flutter wildly.

"Good Lord, woman. You could wake the dead with that caterwauling," James laughed.

"My apologies," she mumbled, keeping her eyes fixed firmly on her cousin. "I was wool-gathering, I'm afraid."

"Flower gathering, too, I see. I'm surprised there are any left with the amount you collect."

James turned to slap Robert on the back.

"It must drive you mad, man."

Abigail chanced a look at Robert to see that he was staring at her with an intensity that caused her heart to stutter.

"I find I don't mind them as much anymore," he

said softly, still gazing at Abigail. "They're growing on me."

Abigail lowered her eyes again and bent to snatch up her basket from the ground, lest she do something mad like throw herself into the man's arms.

She had thought that seeing him again would be embarrassing, yet all she wanted was to be with him. To have him kiss her again.

"Well, once we're in London, you'll be hard pressed to fill your vases, Abby, my dear," James said, oblivious to the undercurrent around him.

The mention of London filled Abby with dismay, and some of what she was feeling must have shown on her face for James threw an arm around her shoulder.

"Don't worry, cousin mine. You'll nab yourself a husband in no time, and you can demand fields of wildflowers from him." He winked.

At the mention of a husband, Abby's eyes foolishly flew to Robert, but he was no longer looking at her.

He was staring at James with an unreadable expression on his face.

He looked...angry?

How strange.

Before she could even begin to try and figure out what had caused his mood to sour, he turned on his heel and walked away. Not sparing a word or a glance for her.

James stared after him with a frown of consternation.

"What happened?" Abigail asked.

James sighed and shook his head slightly before turning to face her.

"I don't know, Abby," he said sombrely. "I thought he was different but—well, maybe some habits are too hard to break."

Before she could question him further, James plucked her basket from her hands.

"Come, I'll walk you back," he said, offering her arm and effectively closing the subject for further discussion.

ROBERT STOMPED BACK to where he and James had tethered their horses, hanging on to his temper by the skin of his teeth.

His behaviour back there had been ridiculous. He knew that. And James would know it. And then he'd have questions that Robert wasn't sure he could answer.

He hated that his first time seeing Abby since the other night had resulted in his storming off in such a way.

But the truth was he'd been craving her company since that evening.

Had looked for her at every meal, only to hear time

and again that she was not feeling well and keeping to her rooms.

Of course, that wasn't true. She was avoiding him.

So, when James had mentioned that he wanted to stop by the fields of wildflowers where she liked to walk in the mornings, Robert hadn't hesitated to agree.

The gentlemen had been intending to go to the village and tie up some of Robert's local business before making the trip to Town next week.

Already, Robert's nerves were shredded. They were to leave Montvale a mere two days before the anniversary of Gina's death.

He'd never spent it away from the Hall before.

But he'd listened when his mother had spoken to him, and he was going to try to remember his sister without drowning in the guilt and horror.

And there was a part of him, too, that knew being around Abigail would be a comfort in itself.

The truth was she made him feel better. She made him want to be a better man.

And so he was braving it. Being amongst the living while he remembered the dead.

He'd found himself anxious to see Abby that morning. To make sure he hadn't scared her off forever.

He had felt like the worst sort of blackguard when she'd been hiding away, knowing that it had been his fault.

And when he'd come upon her, surrounded by her

wildflowers, his heart lifted in a way that frankly terrified him.

It felt as though he could breathe properly for the first time in an age when she'd looked up at him, and he'd suddenly remembered something his mother had said the night they'd had their talk about Gina.

Every morning I open my eyes, and for an infinitesimal moment, I forget why I feel like I can't breathe properly.

Robert had realised with a start that he'd felt exactly like that these last couple of days without Abigail.

Like he couldn't breathe properly.

And before he'd even been able to process what that might mean, James had opened his big mouth and said something about her finding a husband, and Robert's chest had tightened painfully all over again.

For wasn't that why she was here?

Even though she'd come to be such a wonderful part of life at Montvale Hall, befriending his mother, being kind to the servants and villagers, filling the house with her laughter, her scent, her damned flowers, she was only ever supposed to be here temporarily.

She was never going to stay.

She was never going to be his to keep.

The pain of that truth nearly knocked him sideways, and Robert had known that he needed to leave, lest he do something crazy like beg her to stay with him forever.

And that was crazy. Of course it was. Nobody went from soulless monster to willing groom in mere weeks. It was insanity.

He just—he just needed to get the hell away from Abigail Langton until he could trust himself around her again.

Chapter Sixteen

J AMES CAUGHT UP to Robert after he'd run away from Abigail in the meadow. Not something he was proud of, admittedly. When James brought his mount into line with Robert's, Robert felt the other man's stare boring into him.

"Care to explain yourself?" James asked, and though his tone was even enough, Robert heard the underlying anger.

He couldn't blame his best friend. Ironically, if anyone else had spoken to Abby in such a fashion, Robert would have happily put a bullet in him.

Robert took a steadying breath and turned to face his friend.

"I can't," he said simply. And that was the truth. He couldn't because he could barely make sense of his feelings, let alone try to explain them. To Abby's cousin and guardian, of all people.

James studied him for what felt like an age before shaking his head.

"There's only so much of that I'll allow, Robert," he said softly, warning.

Robert wasn't afraid of James, though he had a healthy respect for the man's capabilities.

He was, however, terrified of the fact that James could take Abby from his life forever.

"I'm sorry," he said. It wasn't enough, but it was all he had.

After another brief, intense gaze, James nodded his head, and Robert knew he was forgiven. For now.

"I'd forgotten what it was like to go out in public with you," James said casually as the men rode into the village.

Robert smiled wryly as yet another villager stared at him like he'd grown another head.

"You really are quite famous, aren't you?"

James was tipping his hat to all and sundry, earning himself smiles, bows, and curtsies from everyone.

If Robert touched his hat, they'd probably run screaming, thinking he meant to fling it at them.

They really didn't like him. That was what it came down to.

The rumours that had spread about him over the years, rumours that he was aware of but paid little attention to—well they had him painted as the devil himself. Up there in his big, monstrous house with his poor, long-suffering mother.

Oh, they bowed and curtseyed right enough. He was, after all, the Duke of Montvale and almost single-handedly responsible for the wealth in the village.

It's just that they did so before scarpering as fast as humanly possible.

"You're garnering more attention than I am," Robert answered with a swift smile as he watched the young ladies of the village jostle for position in James's line of vision. "What a thing it is for them to earn a smile from the Angel himself."

James grimaced.

"I hate that name," he sulked. "How come you get something dark, and mysterious, and dangerous? And I get something that makes it sound as though I float around playing a bloody harp?"

"It serves you right," Robert said as he watched from the corner of his eye a mother pull her child behind her.

Had it really come to that? People hiding their children from him?

"How so?" James asked hotly.

"You're too nice," Robert said. "They fawn over you because you're so pleasant all the damned time."

"And they run from you because you're so grumpy all the time," James shot back.

"They run from me because they think I killed my sister," Robert said gruffly. "And with the anniversary of her death approaching, they've no doubt all been discussing it in detail, as they do every year."

James pulled his mount to a sudden halt.

"You're the only one who thinks that, Robert," he

said softly.

Robert didn't want to talk about it. Didn't want to think about it, either, come to that.

His thoughts had been so full of Abigail Langton lately, he barely had room for anything else.

Besides, did he really care what these strangers thought?

In spite of himself, and loathe as he was to admit it, he did care a little.

He hadn't before. But he did now.

And Abigail was responsible for that, too. For try as he might to ignore the thoughts, every so often he imagined her here as his duchess, by his side forever. A ridiculous notion, but one he couldn't shake.

Abigail was so friendly, and according to household gossip, which he pretended not to listen to, she was already beloved in their small Northumberland village.

And for some unfathomable reason, that made Robert wish that he was more liked. Or at least tolerated. Because if Abigail *were* ever to become his duchess, he knew she would want to be involved in village life.

And the only way they'd be able to do that in a manner that she wanted would be if they could travel into the village without everyone running from him and locking their doors.

It was just another reason in the stack of them

piling up that Robert didn't belong with Abigail. Or anyone.

Robert realised that while he was brooding distractedly, again, about Abigail, James was awaiting a response.

But he just didn't have the energy to discuss all of his riotous emotions around Gina's death, and the consequences of it, for the thousandth time. With James or anyone.

Mercifully, James seemed to sense that and with a quick nod, he once more set his mount into motion.

"You know, they'd be less scared of you if you ever actually smiled at one of them," James quipped. "That scowl of yours is enough to turn someone's hair white."

It was foolish in the extreme, but Robert thought of Abigail and found himself actually listening to James.

They came across Mrs. Tellman, the vicar's wife, and rather than give the lady his usual curt nod, Robert made an effort to smile and tip his hat.

Mrs. Tellman's jaw dropped, and she stumbled back, tripping on her skirts and dropping a basket of bread onto the road at her feet.

Robert glowered at James's burst of laughter, as a group of people hurried around and fussed over Mrs. Tellman, helping her to right herself and staring after Robert as though he'd sprouted horns.

"Less scared if I smiled?" he asked with a raised brow.

James's grin was unrepentant.

"It might take some getting used to," he said.

Robert shook his head and reverted to type, scowling and brooding, and wanting to be as far away from other people as possible.

As THE WEEK leading up to their departure progressed, rather than being filled with giddy excitement, a pall of darkness seemed to set over Montvale Hall.

The servants were still going about their business, the same as always.

But James wasn't his usual jovial self, and he'd become very watchful of Abigail and even Robert whenever he was around.

The dowager, too, seemed to be reverting back to the quiet, despondent woman she'd been when Abby had first arrived.

And Robert...

Well, Robert either avoided her like the plague or was quiet and sullen whenever they were around each other.

Abigail felt sick to her stomach as the day of departure drew closer.

This wasn't supposed to have happened to her!

She was supposed to have come here to spend her days shopping and visiting museums, being called upon by gentlemen with posies and sonnets.

These weeks were to have prepared her for a Season so she didn't besmirch her family's name.

She was a Harring on her mother's side, she'd been informed. The niece of the former Marquess of Avondale and cousin to the current one.

The duchess had been wonderful in helping Abby with all sorts of things; the intricate rules of the *haute monde*, the correct style of gown, the complicated and confusing array of titles and addresses for peers and people of quality.

But this week, Abby felt like the lone living creature amongst their small group. And worse, she felt like joining them in the depths of their sorrow. For she would soon have to leave this place. Have to leave Robert.

With a sigh, Abby put down the book she wasn't reading and stood from the chaise.

She'd been in the library all morning, bored and restless and worrying about all manner of things.

Her mind wouldn't be quieted, and she couldn't shake the horrible sense of foreboding. The awful feeling that something bad was coming.

Frustrated with herself for allowing her imagination to run riot, Abby decided she would ride toward the cliffs at the border of Montvale.

But a quick glance out the window put paid to that plan immediately.

The sky was grey and fierce looking. It was the exact colour of Robert's eyes when he was deep in thought, she realised.

It seemed their run of good weather was coming to an end, and it was somehow fitting that the weather should grow steadily more sombre in keeping with the mood of the household.

If going to the beach wasn't feasible, she could at least take a leisurely ride around the estate.

Anything to get out and clear her head.

Mind made up, Abby tried to rally her spirits, and when that didn't work, she figured she might as well be miserable outdoors.

Making her way up to her bedchamber to ring for Bessie, Abby had just taken the first step onto the staircase when she saw Robert coming through the door of his study.

Her heart stopped dead in her chest.

She hadn't seen much of him since that night in his bedroom. Even now, her cheeks heated at the memory.

When she had seen him, he'd been with James, then stomped off in a towering mood about something almost as quickly as he'd arrived.

She hesitated, not knowing if she should call out to him or run away. Not knowing which she'd prefer.

While she was still trying to make up her mind, the decision was taken from her hands.

For at that moment, Robert looked up, his stormy

eyes capturing her own. And she was frozen.

She couldn't have moved if her life depended on it.

"Robert," she breathed, unable to stop her smile of happiness at seeing him.

And at the same time, he spoke.

"Miss Langton."

Abby immediately felt foolish. His tone was so serious. His greeting so formal.

But in the next moment, his expression softened and his eyes grew silvery.

"Abby," he corrected, sounding much less stiff, his gravelly voice sending shivers along her spine.

"I—I was just going to go upstairs," she said, as though it weren't obvious, given she was *on* the stairs.

Heavens! She really did grow idiotic around this man.

And, as was her way in the face of her nervousness, she began to ramble on.

"Of course, you can see that. You don't need me to tell you that. I was going to take a ride around the grounds."

He frowned at her in apparent confusion and instead of stopping her chatter, on she went.

"Well, I was going to ride to the cliffs because I do love it there. It's the sea, you see. Ha! Sea, see."

She paused, but he didn't laugh. Obviously. Because it wasn't bloody funny.

"Anyway, I was going to. But the weather doesn't

look terribly good, and I thought if I was caught in a shower miles away from the Hall, the dowager would have my head. Can you imagine turning up in London at the start of a Season with a fever? So—"

"Abby."

Mercifully, he cut through her waffling with that one simple word.

"Yes?" She swallowed.

"Would you mind if I joined you?"

"Oh." She blinked at him in surprise.

They hadn't been alone since that night.

And really, after what had happened, she should stay as far away from him as humanly possible. And yet, the opportunity to spend time alone with him, especially since it would likely be for the last time, was too good to pass.

"Of course not," she said, a little breathlessly. "I—that would be wonderful."

He smiled an enigmatic smile.

"I'll meet you in the stables in twenty minutes."

He turned on his heel and went back the way he had come, leaving Abby to stare after him.

Her stomach began fluttering madly at the thought of spending time alone with him and the memory of what had happened the last time they'd been alone.

She wondered if it would happen again and was shocked by how much she desperately wanted it to.

Well, there was only one way to find out.

Abby ran up the stairs in a terribly unladylike way.

But she had only twenty minutes, and most of that would be spent trying to calm her nerves.

"DID YOU HAVE a particular location in mind?"

Robert was waiting for her as she entered the stables precisely twenty minutes later, fiddling with the button on her riding glove as she went.

Abigail looked up at his question and saw that he was holding the reins of his stallion, Storm, and the gelding that she'd been using since her arrival.

She'd come to think of the animal as her own but of course, he wasn't hers and after this week, she'd likely never see him again.

A pang of sadness twisted her heart, and it was all Abby could do to keep her countenance as she reached Robert and the horses.

"Not really," she said. "I just wanted to get some air. To clear my mind."

"You have a lot on your mind?" he asked softly.

As a matter of fact, I do, she wanted to say. *Namely, the fact that I am desperately in love with you and am about to go somewhere I don't want to go and meet people I don't want to meet. And I'm not ready to say goodbye to you.*

But that probably wasn't wise.

"I suppose I'm nervous," she said instead. "Going to London, meeting all those new people. Being judged mercilessly wherever I go," she quipped and earned herself a grin.

A groom rushed over with a step for Abby, and she deftly swung herself into the gelding's saddle, trying not to stare as Robert lifted himself onto Storm.

He was so impressive in everything he did. So masculine, so—

"Abby?"

"Yes? What? Yes?"

Great. Not only had he caught her ogling him, but now he was looking at her as though she'd run mad.

"I asked if you were ready."

Rather than answer, she turned her mount and headed out of the stables, desperately trying to get her wits about her as she went.

"You know," Robert's voice sounded casually as he rode up beside her. "I'm surprised to hear that you're nervous about London. You don't strike me as the type of lady who would fear the opinions of Society biddies. Or fear anything, really."

Abigail laughed softly.

"I fear a great many things," she replied. "Rats, for one thing. And yes, even Society biddies. Can you imagine what they'll have to say about an American nobody coming into their folds?"

"Ordinarily, you might be right to be worried,"

Robert said. "But you forget—you will be entering Society with the notorious Monster of Montvale Hall. They'll just be vastly impressed that you managed to survive these past few weeks in my company."

Abigail studied him closely.

He seemed unaffected by what he said, but it pained her to know of his reputation. It was undeserved, she knew now.

Robert was a good man. He loved his mother, was a good friend to James, and an excellent master. His tenants liked and respected him, and he handled his many responsibilities as a duke with poise and equanimity.

He was also, she swallowed hard, almost obscenely handsome. He was strong, and tall, and he smelt divine. Though the Society matrons mightn't put as much store in that as Abby did.

And he was passionate, too. Massively so. Just beneath that stoic surface was a fire that heated her blood with a mere glance.

Yet to the world, he was a monster.

"Why do they call you a monster?" she asked quietly.

In truth, she wasn't sure he'd answer. He wasn't exactly the type to open up and share his feelings.

But he surprised her.

"You will learn that nobody gossips quite like the English upper classes," Robert said dryly. "And I am one of their favourite topics. The fact that I am a duke has me in their sights as it is. But add to that a family tragedy, an abhorrence for socialising, and a less than pleasant demeanour, and you have yourself a monster."

At the casual mention of a family tragedy, Abigail felt her stomach do a little flip-flop. Thus far, the tragedy he spoke of had only been alluded to. Even now, he didn't expand. And she instinctively knew it wasn't something she could question him about.

If he wanted her to know, he would tell her. And the fact that he had mentioned it at all was progress. It meant he was opening up more than ever before. With time, he would hopefully learn to trust her more.

But then, did she even have time? Would they ever get time alone when they got to the busy world of London with all those watchful eyes?

Plus, how likely was it that Robert would go out much in Society at all?

An abhorrence for socialising didn't sound promising. Abigail remembered back to when she'd first arrived at Montvale Hall. How petrified she'd been of the man she'd come to love so very deeply. How arrogant and rude and, yes, frightening he'd been.

But she knew him now. And she knew that just wasn't who he was.

"It seems like an abhorrence for socialising is a good way to keep people from getting too close," she said carefully, watching his reaction.

His eyes snapped to hers, their grey depths expressing first surprise then something so fleeting she could have imagined it. It looked remarkably like tenderness.

Before she could discern it, he'd turned back to face away from her.

"I don't find it as easy to keep people from getting too close as I used to," he said. "I don't find it as easy to want to."

Good Lord.

How Abigail stopped herself from fully launching herself into his arms, she didn't know.

They seemed to be dancing around something here, and it had her nerves fraught.

Could it be that he had come to care for her? And if that were the case, what did that mean for them?

"It's not a weakness, Robert," she said. "Letting people close to you. Letting them see the real you. The man behind the monster."

"Perhaps it's not," he answered. "But old habits die hard, my dear. And I've been alone for many years. Until now."

He looked at her then, and his eyes blazed with silver fire.

Abby drew her horse to a halt, and he did the same.

She should tell him.

She should just tell him how much she had come to care for him. How she loved him.

"You will take them by storm, Abby," he said, his voice coarse. "You will have them all in the palm of your hand."

"I don't want to," she blurted. "I don't want to leave. I'll miss it here so much." She took a deep breath for courage. "I'll miss—"

"Ah, there you are."

Abigail had never sworn overly much but just now, she could have happily rivalled a sailor at James's untimely interruption.

Judging by Robert's suddenly thunderous expression, he felt the same.

"James," he bit out. "Couldn't find anything to occupy yourself?"

"I thought a ride would do me some good," James said, marvellously unperturbed by Robert's evident displeasure. "Where are you two off to?"

Abigail could sense an odd tension between the gentlemen, so she quickly jumped into the conversation.

"I thought perhaps we could go to the river. It's the one part of the estate that I haven't seen, and time is running—"

"No."

Abby stopped in shock as both gentleman simultaneously interrupted her.

She looked from one to the other, taking in their expressions.

James looked worried, and Robert—

Abby couldn't contain a gasp.

Robert looked just as he had when she'd first arrived; furious and ominous.

"I just wanted to see what—"

"Are you deaf? I said, no."

Abby's jaw dropped at Robert's words.

"Robert." James's voice held a thread a steel. "She didn't know."

"How dare you?" she shouted hotly, fuelling the anger that kept the hurt at bay.

Robert glared at her for a moment before suddenly dragging a hand over his face, mumbling an oath.

"Abigail, I'm sorry," he said, and she was surprised by how haggard he looked and sounded. It was like a weight of despair had settled itself over him. "I didn't mean—" He paused then sighed and shook his head. "I'm sorry."

Without another word, he turned his horse and shot off across the grounds as fast as the wind.

"What on earth?" Abby turned to James.

She knew what he would say before he even spoke.

"It's not—"

"Your story to tell," she finished bleakly.

Without another word, she turned her horse and rode off, making sure she went the opposite direction as Robert.

Chapter Seventeen

THE DAY BEFORE their admittedly miserable party's departure for London, the heavens opened and a storm raged.

In fact, the weather was almost as bleak as the mood in the house.

Since the bizarre episode the previous day, Robert had kept his distance. From Abigail, and from everyone else.

He didn't join them for meal times. It was like he'd disappeared. And only the servants' fearful expressions and hushed countenances were evidence of his presence.

The dowager had grown steadily more morose, as well, and none of Abigail's efforts to rouse the woman's spirits had any sort of effect.

Even James couldn't muster more than a fleeting smile for her.

Abigail had no idea what had happened to make everyone steadily more miserable as the days went on, but it was becoming untenable.

She felt as if she were slowly losing her mind, surrounded as she was by so much unexplained grief.

James was the only other living being she'd seen who would actually speak more than a few words to her, save for Bessie.

They'd shared an almost silent meal that morning to break their fast. A meal that nobody else had turned up to.

Luncheon was ignored by everyone but Abigail and rather than sit alone at a giant table, she returned to her room and requested a tray.

Now it was approaching the dinner hour, and Abigail had no idea if she should go downstairs for it, or who she would see, or what would happen.

It was most unsettling.

Finally, after writing to both of her sisters, unpacking and repacking her trunks, and twiddling her thumbs for a considerable amount of time, she decided that she would dress and go down to dinner.

After all, it was to be her last night in Northumberland. And while that depressing thought did nothing to lift her mood, it was enough to convince her not to hide herself away.

She rang for Bessie to fill a hot, lavender-scented bath and instructed the maid to lay out her sky-blue silk gown.

Maybe it was foolish, but she couldn't help hoping that Robert would be there, and she wanted to look as good as possible before she had to leave Montvale Hall, and him, behind.

"Forgive me, your grace. Your mother has sent word that she will dine in her rooms this evening."

Robert clenched his jaw as the butler delivered the softly-spoken missive.

He gave the servant a quick nod of acknowledgement, but did not speak as the older gentleman bowed then glided from the room.

It was laughable, really, that he'd accused the duchess of forgetting Gina's death.

All week, as her anniversary had loomed, Robert had withdrawn further into himself, so it should be no surprise that his mother had done the same.

James had been hanging around him all week, forcing his company on Robert, refusing to be put off by snarls, shouts, or anything else Robert could throw at him.

It had always been thus; this time of year he would want nothing more than to surrender to the darkness, and James, Simon, Nicholas, or all three together would pop up and refuse to leave him alone.

This year, Simon had to travel to Town early, and Nicholas was handling some crisis or other in Ireland or Robert knew they would have been here, along with James, annoying the hell out of him.

The truth was, however, that this year the level of darkness that consumed him almost came as a shock.

And he knew the reason why.

Abigail.

Ever since she'd stormed into his life like a blue-eyed, blonde-haired hurricane, his very existence had turned upside down.

And whether he had wanted it to or not, his mood had lifted, his heart had begun to beat again, and his world brightened.

That just made his grief now seem that much blacker. Because he hadn't been wallowing in misery these past few weeks.

He'd felt something akin to happiness. He'd experienced lightness. He'd laughed, and he'd—

Robert stopped that thought before it was allowed to form and knocked back the tumbler filled with brandy that he'd been nursing whilst he'd brooded.

But his mind would not be silenced.

He'd loved.

Really, truly loved.

He loved Abigail Langton so much that it took his breath away.

What was it that his mother had said?

When you loved someone, a piece of your soul became theirs.

And Robert felt like his soul had split clean down the middle, and half of it was irrevocably and irretrievably in the hands of Abby.

The part that belonged to her was the part that had remembered how to love, and laugh, and live again.

That wanted to fill every room in the house with her wildflowers, just to see her smile.

That wanted to listen to her ramble on about birds kissing and Society biddies gossiping.

That wanted him to take her in his arms and never let her go.

For a brief, mad moment, Robert felt like doing just that.

But he stopped himself in time.

Filling his glass yet again, he shook his head at his own idiocy.

For the blackened part of his soul that still lingered inside him knew that it was no use.

He hadn't even told Abigail what it was that tormented him so.

He hadn't confessed that he'd as good as killed his sister. And while he might be able to believe that his father's death wasn't on his hands, nobody could convince him that Gina's wasn't.

What right did he have to take something as pure, and light, and loving as Abby's heart, and entwine it with his own poisoned organ?

The monster that she claimed didn't exist was always there inside him, lurking and waiting to drag him into the hell of memory and guilt.

He could never drag Abby in there with him. And he knew that's exactly what would happen.

With her courage and strength and capacity for love, she would stick it out with him, no matter how tormented he became.

And then what would become of her? Would he make her a shell of the woman she'd once been, like he'd done to his mother?

Would he let her down somehow, in some way, that would put her in danger, like Gina?

Or would he drive her to do something tragic, like his father?

The truth was that anyone who'd ever loved him and gotten close to him had ended up broken at his hands.

And whilst somehow he got himself out of bed every morning to fight his demons for another day, he knew that if anything happened to Abby it would be the thing that finally broke him beyond repair.

Robert refreshed his glass once more.

He was in his cups, he knew, and well on the way to being thoroughly foxed.

That would make tomorrow's arduous journey toward London significantly more difficult.

Especially if the weather kept up like this; there was no way he would be able to travel on horseback.

As though his thoughts had awoken the storm, just then a flash of lightning illuminated the sky, and not three seconds later, the thunder bellowed loud enough to rattle the windowpanes of his study.

The storm was raging fiercely.

How tragically ironic that the weather should be so similar to the weather all those years ago.

He'd lost his baby sister during that storm. And he was going to lose the woman he loved during this.

It wasn't fair.

Though perhaps it was.

Perhaps he was finally getting a punishment to fit the crime of allowing Gina to drown all those years ago.

Because Robert could think of nothing worse than having to live a hollow life without Abby.

Chapter Eighteen

"I'M GLAD TO have some company for dinner, at least." Abby smiled across the table at her cousin, who was making a valiant effort to keep her entertained.

The dowager had sent her apologies.

Robert had sent no such message. He just hadn't shown up.

James attempted to return her smile, but it was more a grimace, and he was as sombre as ever she'd seen him.

"I apologise, Abby," he said gravely. "I shouldn't have brought you here. Not now. I thought that perhaps if the dowager had something else to focus on. I even thought Robert—"

He stopped and shook his head, and Abby had to clench her fists to prevent herself from reaching out and shaking him.

You thought Robert, what? She wanted to yell. But of course, she did no such thing.

"I must confess myself confused about everyone's behaviour," she hedged carefully. "I have felt like a ghost these past days, floating around a seemingly empty house."

James sighed.

"I know, and I am more sorry for that than I can say. Truth be told, I've been spending a lot of time with Robert trying to—well, I don't know, trying to undo the damage of the last fifteen years."

He laughed self-deprecatingly.

"I even thought for a while there that you might be the one thing to bring him out of his depression."

Abigail's stomach twisted painfully.

"Now, I'm quite sure nothing will," James finished.

Her eyes filled with tears, and she rapidly blinked them away.

Yes, it hurt to hear James essentially say that he didn't see Robert feeling anything for her. But being a watering pot wouldn't do her any good now.

"James." She leaned over and clasped her cousin's hand.

He'd been like a brother to her ever since he'd arrived in New York.

But Robert and James had been friends since childhood. And they'd obviously been through something huge together.

Bonds like that were difficult to break, and if James didn't want to break Robert's confidence, then she would be no closer to finding out the truths behind the mystery.

"Please, tell me what I can do. I want to help him."

James studied her intently, as though he were sizing her up.

The tension was unbearable.

It was time she was honest. With him at least.

"I care about him. I want to help."

"Oh, Abby."

There was a world of sympathy in James's voice, and Abigail wasn't entirely sure she was happy about it.

As though he felt sorry for someone in such a hopeless situation as she.

"I confess, watching you both the last couple of weeks, I began to hope you *could* help him. I probably should have been a better guardian. Watched you more closely. But Robert—well, the difference in him—I had thought…" He trailed off. "I don't suppose there's any hope for him."

Abigail felt inexplicably angry.

Angry that James would say such a thing about Robert; that he'd be trapped in this miserable hell forever.

Angry that nobody would tell her *why* he was trapped like this.

Angry that she would have to leave here tomorrow, and her last days had been miserable.

Because she knew she didn't want to leave.

In spite of all the bad—the black humours, the mysteries, the monster—she loved Robert so much she couldn't bear the thought of him never being able to let go of what haunted him.

And suddenly, she'd had enough.

She wasn't going to scurry off to London in the company of a man who was in this much pain and hated Society, as it was.

She wasn't going to drag the duchess around the bright lights of the Season, whilst she nursed such a dreadful sorrow.

Most of all, she wasn't going to sit idly by while the man she loved suffered alone.

Perhaps she couldn't help.

But she could try.

Standing from her chair, filled with fresh determination, Abigail looked at James with a confidence she didn't feel.

She was quaking in her satin slippers.

But that was neither here nor there.

"If you'll excuse me," she said, turning to leave before he had the chance to stop her.

"Abby, wait."

"No!" she called over her shoulder as she rushed from the room.

"Abigail. Stop."

James's voice rang out sternly across the dining hall, and his shouting was such a rare occurrence that it served to halt her movements.

She spun round to face her cousin.

"This isn't something you should involve yourself in. Robert finds it—difficult—to let people in."

"We're leaving for London tomorrow, James. And once we're there, Robert never has to speak to me again, should he not wish to. What do I have to lose?"

James seemed to be struggling internally before finally releasing a breath.

"All right," he said quietly, simply.

Abigail offered him a small smile before turning and rushing from the room.

Perhaps telling Robert what was in her heart would enable him to open his own.

ROBERT LIFTED HIS head at the sound of the timid knock on his study door.

Quite how he'd heard it over the cacophony of noises from the storm raging outside was beyond him. But heard it he did.

And he knew it was Abigail. Somehow, he had known she would come.

He didn't bother calling out for her to enter. She would do just as she pleased anyway.

He smiled a little at the thought of the wilful woman who would no doubt come marching into the room and demand answers.

How would he ever be able to give them to her?

As he'd suspected, the door creaked open and then, there she was.

A vision in blue. A blue that made her eyes impossibly deep pools of azure.

Deep enough to drown in.

The irony wasn't lost on him, and he almost groaned aloud from the lance of pain to his heart.

Robert watched as she stepped closer. Not marching. Her movements were hesitant, as though she were afraid of something. Afraid of him.

She was probably right to be.

"Miss Langton."

The words sounded slurred, even to his own ears.

He had certainly followed in his father's footsteps this night. And like his father, had found no comfort in the bottom of a brandy bottle.

Watching her as closely as he was, he saw the hurt flash across her eyes, presumably at his formal greeting.

But he was losing her tomorrow. Had never really had her to begin with. So why not keep his distance now?

"We missed you at dinner," she said softly, the light from the fire and candles lighting her golden curls and making her look impossibly innocent and lovely.

"I wasn't hungry," he drawled, feigning a nonchalance that he didn't feel.

"But you were clearly thirsty," Abigail quipped,

eyeing the empty bottle on the table quizzically.

He made no attempt to stand to greet her, choosing instead to stay just as he was; sprawled across the deuced uncomfortable chaise in only his linen shirt.

If his bad manners or state of dishabille shocked Abby, however, she gave no indication of it.

"I came to check if you were well." She finally spoke again when he made no response to her remark.

He laughed then. A bitter, ugly sound.

"If I am well? Sweetheart, I haven't been well for years."

"Oh? And why is that?" she asked boldly, and God help him but he loved her all the more for it.

"That," he said slowly, if not clearly, "is none of your damned business."

He saw the sharp intake of breath rather than heard it. It was getting increasingly hard to hear anything over the gales and lashing rain outside.

He wondered what she would do in the face of his cruelty. Cry? Yell at him? Turn and run from the big, bad monster?

But he should have known Abby would keep surprising him.

For she stood still and raised her chin defiantly.

Robert lifted his tumbler to his mouth before realising it was empty.

With a black oath, he stood unsteadily from the couch, and staggered to his drinks table.

He kept his back to Abigail as he sloshed some amber liquid into the glass, not offering one to her.

"Robert, please. I want—"

"You know," he cut across her, his tone conversational. "Unless you want to destroy your reputation within the first five minutes of your arrival in London, you really must learn not to address a Peer so informally. Show a little decorum."

He turned to face her in time to see her recoil as if he'd slapped her.

A part of him, the part that still resembled something human, railed against him for hurting her.

He was an utter bastard, he knew.

But he couldn't stop himself from being cruel.

If he hurt her now with his words, he couldn't hurt her in the future with his actions.

Abby's eyes flashed blue fire.

Ah, he'd awakened her temper.

But rather than yell at him or stomp out the door, which he wanted and didn't, she again stood her ground.

"I wouldn't address any other Peer so informally," she said evenly, her voice clear and strong, save for the slightest tremor. "Only you."

Robert fought desperately to ignore the bricks tumbling from the wall around his heart.

A particularly loud clap of thunder rent the air, and he flinched, remembering how loud it had been that night. The night before his fingers had let go of Gina's.

"I'm a duke, Miss Langton. I deserve more decorum than the rest of them put together."

His voice dripped with disdain, he knew.

I'm sorry, he was saying frantically in his head. *I'm so sorry, my love. I want you to leave, but God how I need you to stay.*

"You're not a duke to me." She stepped forward suddenly, and he felt the mad urge to step back. But of course he didn't. "You're Robert. You're the man I—"

"Be that as it may," he cut across her arrogantly, "I *am* a duke. And you would do well to mind your manners in Town."

"Damn it, we're not *in* Town." Finally, the cracks were starting to show. He'd never heard her swear like that. He probably shouldn't find it endearing, yet he did.

She stomped toward him, closing the distance so there were only inches between them.

She was close enough to touch. Yet so very far away from him.

"I shall behave perfectly respectably in your precious Town."

Her eyes were filling with tears and he knew if they fell, so too would the last of his defences.

"Best not to let them know about the liberties you allow men to take with you then, sweetheart. You'll get yourself a reputation."

Abby's hand shot out and cracked across his cheek.

Immediately she looked contrite, covering her mouth with the same hand.

"Why are you doing this?" A lone tear slipped down her cheek, and he had to clench his fists to keep from reaching for her.

"It's better this way," he ground out.

"No," she insisted. "How can this be better? Locking yourself away, drinking yourself to oblivion. Hiding from the people who care about you. This isn't better."

Her words were like lances. The truth hurt, he supposed.

"What the hell would you know about it?" he snarled. "You have no idea what you're talking about."

He spun away from her to glare at the storm outside the window.

"I know you," she insisted.

God, but she was tenacious.

"And this isn't you."

Robert's emotions threatened to spin out of control.

"You *don't* know me," he roared, and she blanched, stumbling back a few steps and making him feel sick for scaring her.

"Yes, I do," she cried stubbornly, even as the tears ran unchecked down her face. "You are not this man."

"You're not wrong there, sweetheart." He made the endearment sound like a filthy oath. "I am this monster. Haven't all the locals and servants been telling you that? Haven't I?"

She pressed her hands to her temples, shaking her head.

"I don't know why you're doing this. Why won't you tell me what's wrong? I can help. I want to help."

"You can't help me. Nobody can."

"I can," she repeated. "Please, talk to me. Please, let me in."

He clenched his jaw to keep from roaring his frustrations at her.

The storm grew louder and crueller outside, and the memories were slamming into him, making his head pound.

"Talk to me," she demanded, and finally, his control snapped.

"And tell you *what?*" he yelled. "What would you like to talk about, Abby? The fact that I killed my baby sister?"

This time he heard her gasp, even over the racket outside.

The wind was howling now, hurtling through the cavernous house, crying out like a lost soul.

It seemed like eons that they stood there, facing each other like combatants across a war field.

Abigail broke the deafening silence first.

"That can't be true," she whispered. But he saw it in her eyes; the fear of the monster. And it was more than he could stand.

"It's true," he rasped.

"Well then, it—it must have been an accident. You wouldn't do anything to hurt someone you care about."

I'm hurting you.

"You don't understand. You don't know me."

"I know you," she said softly. And the tenderness in her voice, even coupled with the apprehension, nearly brought him to his knees. "Robert, I love you."

For one, brief moment, Robert's heart burst with elation and he moved to reach for her, to pull her into his arms and tell her how much he loved her, too.

But reality reared its ugly head.

How could she love he who was unlovable?

He could only stare at her whilst the storm swirled outside and within.

He saw the moment that her heart broke at his silence; her face crumpled, and the tears came again.

"Your sister." She spoke again.

"Don't," he warned.

He couldn't stand to have Abigail speak about Gina.

"I want to understand."

He shook his head.

"Just get out, Abigail," he said wearily, his anger

simmering, waiting to explode.

"But if you tell me what happened…"

Damn it. She wouldn't bloody listen.

His anger erupted, awakening the monster in him like never before.

"I said, GET OUT."

His voice ricocheted around the room, loud enough to compete with the clamorous thunder, and it worked like nothing else had.

With a cry of distress, Abby turned and ran from him.

"I'm sorry," he whispered as she ran.

But of course, it was too late.

She was gone.

Chapter Nineteen

A FEAR AND despair unlike anything she'd ever known coursed through Abby's veins, making it impossible for her to think straight.

She would never say that Robert was capable of hurting her. Even when he'd roared at her, a part of her knew she was in no real danger. Not physically, at least.

Emotionally, he had torn her to shreds.

Her heart was pounding. So, too, was her head.

Abby ran blindly, no direction in mind. She just needed to get away from him. From this house, where it suddenly felt like the walls were closing in on her.

Reaching the dining hall, she looked up and through her tears saw the blurry image of James emerging from the room.

"Abigail," he called. "What happened?"

But she didn't stop. She couldn't.

Darting past James, ignoring his calls, she ran straight through the Hall to the conservatory and from there, straight out into the storm.

The rain pelted against the bare skin exposed by her short-sleeved gown and within seconds, the garment was soaked, as were the matching slippers.

But she didn't care.

Her mind was teeming with hundreds of riotous thoughts, her heart swirling with painful emotion after painful emotion.

She couldn't breathe past the pain, couldn't think past the turmoil.

She needed space and freedom and to be as far from Robert as she could get.

So, on she ran. Her only goal being some much-needed distance.

"WHAT THE HELL happened in here?"

Robert winced as James's furious question drilled into his pounding head.

He should have expected the other man's anger.

What he'd done to Abby just now was unforgiveable.

All he wanted was to find her and beg for her forgiveness.

But of course, he wouldn't do that. For one thing, he loved her too much to allow her to saddle herself with a man like him.

For another, if James's livid demeanour was anything to go by, he probably wasn't going to make it out of this room alive.

Robert looked at James, who glared right back.

This man was his oldest and closest friend. He'd been there through the worst time in Robert's life, along with Simon and Nicholas. And they were all still there, waiting in the wings of his existence, always ready to come back into his life in a real way, should he want them to.

He'd never wanted them to.

He'd never wanted anyone.

Until now.

"Well?" James prompted, and Robert realised he hadn't answered his friend.

He also couldn't remember what he'd asked.

Turning from where he'd been studying the fire in the grate, Robert prepared for a long, likely very loud, conversation.

"What?" he bit out.

James's glower deepened at Robert's tone but instead of railing against him, which Robert had expected, his friend sighed and silently turned to close the study door before facing Robert once more.

"We need to talk," he said sombrely, and immediately, Robert's defences went up.

"Everyone feels like talking this evening," he drawled sarcastically.

James ignored him.

He walked to the table holding the pitiful remnants of Robert's brandy and raised a brow.

"I was going to suggest a drink but perhaps not," he quipped.

Coming back to the chaise in front of the fireplace, James sat down.

He leaned his elbows on his knees and sat forward, looking gravely at the still-standing duke.

"I told Abby it was a bad idea to go anywhere near you today."

"But she didn't listen," Robert guessed wryly, even managing the tiniest of smiles.

Typical Abby.

"No, she didn't. And she's ended up in tears, running as though—"

"As though she were being chased by a monster?" Robert finished, bitterness lacing his words with venom.

"I've been understanding, Robert. More than anyone else." James stood, and Robert could feel the tension coming off the marquess in waves. "I've indulged your moods for years. Tolerated your depressions, tried to help with your misplaced guilt."

Misplaced? Had everyone just forgotten what Robert had done?

Before he could argue, however, James continued.

"But I'm not going to stand idly by while Abby becomes collateral damage."

Robert clenched his jaw but refused to give any other indication that James's words were affecting him.

God, even the mention of her name hurt.

"I was foolish, I suppose, to allow Abigail to get as close to you as she did. But you seemed almost…happy with her. And I could see how much she was growing to care for you."

"Well then, you should have stopped that," Robert cut in defensively. He didn't like where this conversation was headed. "You should have known better than to let her anywhere near me."

He wasn't going to comment on what James had said about his feelings for Abigail, because he was too close to the truth for comfort.

"The fact that you think I could stop Abby from doing anything proves you don't know her very well," James said.

He was wrong, but Robert didn't bother arguing.

"But why shouldn't I let her near you? You have a good heart, Robert."

His words were eerily like his cousin's before him.

"And I thought Abby could succeed where the rest of us failed."

Robert swallowed hard past the lump in his throat.

He was sobering up by the second, and the thought of how he'd treated Abby was turning his stomach.

He was every bit the monster people claimed he was.

"But clearly, she hasn't. And now, she's run off in tears, and I wish to God I'd never brought her here."

Robert was about to say he wished Abigail hadn't come here, too. But he stopped himself.

Why lie to his oldest friend?

He didn't wish Abby hadn't come. He just wished he was worthy of her.

"I'm going to find her," he said, suddenly desperate to apologise.

But before he took his first step, James was off the sofa.

"You're not going anywhere near her," he said softly.

It was only then that Robert noticed his friend's clenched jaw and fists.

James was hanging onto his temper by sheer force of will, it would seem.

The two friends hadn't come to blows since their childhood when it seemed of the four of them, two were always fighting about some event or another.

Yet in that moment, James looked like he could happily beat Robert to a pulp. Or try, at least.

And Robert knew he deserved it. But there would be time enough for that later. Right now, he wanted to get to Abby.

"I'm going to find her, James," he repeated. "I need to apologise."

"Damn it, Rob. She doesn't *need* your apologies," James yelled. "She needs you to stay the hell away from her. And that includes London. I don't want you coming. I don't want you anywhere near her."

Robert felt a wave of fury swamp him at James's words.

Nobody was going to keep him from the woman he loved.

Except you.

The inner thought brought him up short.

Hadn't that been his motivation for treating Abigail so abominably? To keep her away from him?

To let her go and live her life with someone whose heart wasn't black and mangled?

Yet hearing it from James, knowing that in a few short weeks she was likely to have found some such person, a possessiveness like he'd never felt before slammed into Robert.

He couldn't stand by while someone else claimed her heart.

Selfish cad that he was, he couldn't do it.

"James." He forced his tone to stay patient, even. "I'm sorry for what I did to Abby."

James's eyes widened then narrowed furiously.

"If you put your hands on her, I'll—"

"What? Of course, I didn't put my bloody hands on her," Robert interrupted angrily. "How could you even think that?"

An unwanted imagine of he and Abigail in his bedchamber the other night flashed in Robert's mind, but he pushed it away.

James thought Robert had touched her in anger, in violence. The idea made him sick. And he didn't want the memory of the other night sullied with the ugliness of this evening.

When Abigail left, his memories would be the only thing he had left of her.

"How could I not?" James threw back, though he sounded relieved. "She was beside herself leaving here. And in fact, I've wasted far too much time in here trying to get anything through your thick skull. I'm going to check on her. Just because you don't care about her, doesn't mean I don't."

James turned and began to move swiftly from the room.

"James."

Robert's voice stopped him.

James turned back and raised a brow, waiting for Robert to speak.

"I care," Robert said simply, quietly.

James studied him for what seemed an age, and Robert felt inexplicably nervous.

Finally, his friend nodded. "Let's go and find her then," he said.

Chapter Twenty

ABIGAIL WAS SOAKED to the bone and shivering.
Perhaps running from the Hall into a storm wearing nothing but a silk evening gown hadn't been the cleverest of ideas.

But she hadn't been thinking clearly.

All she had wanted, desperately needed, in fact, was space from Robert.

She had told him that she loved him. And he had thrown her out.

The rejection stung, but that wasn't what hurt the most.

No, the sharp, twisting pain was her heart breaking into a million pieces, she was sure. For not only did he not say the words back, but Abigail knew now that he never would.

She hadn't believed him when he had said he was incapable of love.

But she believed him now.

Believed him because when she'd looked into his stormy grey eyes, all she'd seen was desolation and coldness. No trace of love, or warmth, or even humanity had lurked in their depths.

And that was what she'd run from.

Now she was out in a raging storm, scared and freezing, and regretting her flight.

She shielded her eyes from the driving rain as best she could, whilst the howling wind battered her from all sides.

It was too dark to see clearly, so Abigail couldn't be sure where she even was on the grounds, and the sporadic flashes of lightning weren't much help.

Deciding to head back the way she'd come and just hide in her rooms until they were to travel tomorrow, Abigail turned to trek back to the house.

She didn't want to see Robert again.

She didn't really believe he'd killed his sister…did she?

No, of course not!

Besides, James had said there'd been a childhood tragedy. Which meant that whatever had befallen Robert's sister had happened when he'd been a child himself.

Despite her anger, and even despite her better judgment, Abigail felt a pang of sympathy for Robert.

What sort of terrible burden had the man been carrying for all these years?

Was it any wonder that he was so closed off from the world?

Abigail drew to a stop as her confusing thoughts bombarded her.

What had she come to? Worrying about Robert in the middle of a raging storm. It was ridiculous, even for her.

Her mother had always said her impetuous behaviour would land her in trouble. And it looked as though she had been right.

In the midst of her despair, the sound of thundering water caught Abigail's attention.

It had been impossible to hear anything above the wind and thunder up until now, but it seemed as though the storm was starting to die down a little. Even the rain was easing up, making other sounds easier to hear.

Abigail turned toward the sound and began to make her way toward it. It was still too dark to see clearly, but her eyes had adjusted to the darkness enough to make out the shapes and shadows around her.

The river!

She had come as far as the river and as she inched closer, she could see that the storm had swelled the water, making it seem close to bursting its banks.

The river that she'd wanted to see, yet hadn't ever come to.

That she saw from the corner window in her bedchamber and was always curious about.

The river that had for some reason caused such an explosive reaction from Robert.

Abigail walked closer still, until she came to a tree

whose branches hung over the teeming water.

She leaned against the trunk and sank slowly to the sodden river bank.

She was already cold and soaking. Her dress was already ruined. And she was too exhausted, mentally and physically, to do anything other than sit on the river bank and cry.

The wind picked up again, and the rain began to lash heavier than ever. The storm hadn't abated then, it had tricked her into thinking it was softening.

Well, the storm and the man who'd stolen her heart had that in common.

ROBERT'S UNEASINESS GREW steadily toward full-scale panic, but he refused to give the emotion any chance to overwhelm him. Instead, brutally pushing it aside.

They'd looked everywhere in the house.

Even the duchess had been roused from her sleep, though they'd known there was no way Abby had would have gone into that particular bedchamber.

But then, where the hell was she?

"What do we do?" He turned toward James, desperation in his voice.

James looked worried sick, which didn't help Robert's panic.

"I don't know. She—perhaps she just refuses to see

you?"

Robert didn't think Abigail was the type to hide away and pretend not to be in the house.

She was far too courageous for that.

But then, she'd never been treated so abominably, he was sure.

"Bring Miss Langton's maid to us, again," James called to a waiting footman before facing Robert again.

"We'll tell the maid that we just want to know Abby is all right. If she doesn't want to—Robert! Where are you going?"

Robert ignored James's surprised shout as he bolted from the room.

He couldn't stand idly by while Abigail's maid shook and stammered in front of him again, barely getting a word out.

If Abigail was hiding in her room, then he needed to apologise. He wouldn't bother her. If she truly wanted to be left alone then he would respect that.

But, God, he needed to say sorry. He needed to see that she was there.

Finally reaching the door to Abby's bedchamber, Robert knocked gently at first, then pounded his fist against the wood, panic making his limited patience wafer-thin.

"Abby?" he called, uncaring of the audience he had amassed.

James, the dowager, and even the footman who'd been sent to find Abby's maid were all watching him, each looking alarmed.

The door opened, and Robert's knees nearly gave out with relief.

But it wasn't Abigail standing there. It was her terrified-looking maid, yet again.

"Is she here?" he demanded, knowing that he sounded every inch the imperious duke.

"N-no, your grace," the maid stuttered. "Tis like I said earlier, Miss Langton hasn't been back since before dinner."

Without another word, Robert slipped past the girl and into the bedchamber, ignoring his mother's cries of disapproval.

Abby had to be in here. She just had to be.

The alternative was that she was missing. Because of him.

His eyes darted around the room, taking in the truth of the maid's words.

Bed made, night rail laid out, fire crackling in the hearth. But no Abigail.

"Robert, really, you cannot come into a lady's bed-chamber."

"Any sign of her?"

His mother's and James's questions demanded his attention, but Robert ignored them both as his panic threatened to consume him.

He turned from them to look unseeingly out the windows.

The storm outside appeared to be dying down, but

the one ravaging him on the inside was kicking up stronger than ever.

She couldn't have gone outside in the storm, could she? Surely, she wouldn't endanger herself like that?

A crack of lightning illuminated the grounds, and Robert caught sight of the merest flash of sky blue. A colour that didn't belong outside in the world of greys, and blacks, and shadows.

He pressed his hands against the windowpane, his eyes desperately scanning the grounds below.

The river was visible from here, looking as monstrous as it had the night Gina had died.

Robert's palms grew sweaty, his heart racing.

No. Surely not. Surely the fates wouldn't be so cruel as to have led Abigail to the place of his darkest nightmares.

"Did you see that?"

His voice sounded haggard, spent.

"What?" James rushed to his side. "What did you see?"

Rather than answer, Robert's entire focus remained on the landscape outside.

Had he imagined it?

A crack of lightning lit up the sky again.

There!

That flash of blue again.

It was Abigail. It had to be.

And she was headed straight for the river.

Fear, unlike any he'd experienced since his childhood, slammed into Robert and without another thought for James or anything else, Robert turned on his heel and ran from the room.

His mind raced and roiled with tumultuous thoughts.

Abigail was outside in a storm, alone. And she was at the one place Robert had vowed he'd never go.

But how could he not go back there? When he knew that was where she was.

He heard the shouts behind him; James and his mother calling to him and calling out instructions to servants as they chased after him.

Yet nothing was going to slow him down. Nothing was going to stop him.

He had to get to Abigail.

Robert burst through the conservatory doors that were closest to the river, and immediately he was soaked to the bone.

Abigail would catch her death of cold in this.

She didn't have a dinner jacket to offer at least some protection. Or the better part of a bottle of brandy sloshing around her insides to keep her warm.

Has it really only been an hour ago I'd been unable to string a sentence together? Robert thought distractedly. He'd never felt so sober in his life.

Determined to get to Abigail, to get her inside and safe, Robert pushed through the driving rain and violent wind.

But as he got closer to the riverbank, another insidious fear began to slither through Robert's veins.

A sinister and old one, one that had never released him from its clutches. It had always been there inside him, dormant save for the control it had over his life, forcing him into isolation, forcing him to push away anyone he'd ever loved.

Now, though, it was coursing through him, filling him with the same blind panic that had made him stand frozen on the riverbank for those few, life-changing seconds all those years ago.

He was close enough now to hear the thunderous water of the river. It was almost as loud as his thumping heart.

Another flash of lightning, and there she was, huddled by the same tree that Gina had fallen from.

Oh, God.

"Abby!" he managed to shout, even as panic clawed at his throat and stole the breath from his lungs.

But she'd heard.

He watched as her head lifted and turned toward him.

Watched as she scrambled to her feet.

Though he couldn't hear her voice, he watched her mouth open in surprise then form his name.

And he watched as the muddy riverbank gave away to the riotous waters, and Abigail slipped and fell toward the river.

Chapter Twenty-One

T IME STOOD STILL, just as it had on the day Gina had died.

This couldn't be happening again.

Was life really so very cruel as that?

How could he possibly watch this woman die?

All these thoughts tumbled over each other in Robert's head as Abigail disappeared from view.

But this time, there was no one else to force him into action.

Just him.

And he wasn't going to lose Abby.

With a roar of frustration, he closed the distance to the river.

Please, please, please, God, he begged over and over as he ran. *Please, don't take her from me. Please, don't let her die.*

Robert thought he heard shouting from behind him, but he didn't stop to check.

All he wanted was to get to Abigail.

If she was in the water, if she'd been swept away, then his life would end there and then on the riverbank.

He skidded to a halt where Abby had fallen, and with a dread that almost made him cast up his accounts, he leaned over the edge to peer down to the river.

"Robert!"

Robert's knees gave out with relief, and he sank to the ground.

Abby had slipped, yes. But she hadn't gone into the water.

She was covered in muck and shivering. But she wasn't in the water.

"I-I've twisted my ankle, I think," she called miserably.

He watched her speak, heard her words, but he couldn't seem to move.

His fear and relief, his love and guilt, and regret, they were swirling inside him, and he didn't know how to react to any one of them, so he simply stared at her.

"Are you going to help me?" she demanded hotly. And it was so very like her to be sitting, covered in mud in the middle of a storm, yet ordering him about as though she were a queen, that he couldn't help his burst of laughter.

She narrowed those beautiful blue eyes.

"It's *not* funny," she snarled. "My dress is ruined."

And Robert laughed harder.

She'd almost died. But she was worried about her

dress.

And God, but he loved her more in that moment than ever before.

With a huff, she staggered to her feet.

But the second she put her weight on her bad ankle, she stumbled back toward the water.

Her eyes widened in fear, but Robert's hands shot out and grabbed hold of her, pulling her up the embankment and against him, then wrapping her in as tight a hold as he could manage, while still allowing her to breathe.

Robert sat on the soaked, muddy ground safely distanced from the riverbank, and just held her.

And it felt glorious.

She was here. Safe and *alive* and in his arms. And nothing had ever felt so wonderful. So right.

He rained kisses down upon her head then moved his hands to clasp either side of her face, pulling back so he could study her.

"Are you hurt?" he demanded, his voice quivering with so many things. "Aside from your ankle."

Abby was staring at him as though he were a confusing specimen in a museum.

"Abby," he prompted, shaking her gently. "Are you hurt?"

"N-n-no," she managed, and he realised then that her teeth were chattering, and the trembling he felt wasn't just from him but from her body that was wracked with shivers.

"Dammit," he muttered.

He stood with her still in his arms and placed her gently on her feet while still supporting her.

Without a word, he stripped himself of his jacket and wrapped it around her.

It was soaking, so it probably wouldn't do much good. But it had to be better than nothing, didn't it?

A whole new set of worries bombarded him.

What if she caught a fever from this? What if the fever killed her? That would be his fault, too.

Robert felt sick when he thought of how much pain she must be in with her ankle, and all because he'd sent her running out into a storm.

But he could indulge in self-pitying guilt later.

For now, he needed to get her home and warm.

The rain was pelting them, causing his linen shirt to stick to him, and he watched as Abby's eyes travelled over his chest and back to meet his own.

When she saw that he was watching, her cheeks flamed brightly enough for him to notice, even in the dark.

And even though they'd resolved nothing, even though he was worried sick about her, even though he'd probably scared her witless enough to have lost her forever, some part of him responded to her blushes in a way that was entirely inappropriate. But oh, so tempting.

And despite the dire situation, an imp of mischief awoke in him.

"Now is hardly the time to be ogling me, Abby." He frowned with mock severity.

Her jaw dropped, and her eyes flashed blue fire.

"I was not," she shouted, hotly. "I was just—you were, that is, I hadn't—"

He couldn't help it. She was a temptress without even realising it.

Robert bent his head and captured her lips in a brief, hard kiss.

With any luck, there would be plenty of time to beg her forgiveness and to kiss her senseless in the future.

Right now, she needed to be inside.

Without another word, he bent and lifted her into his arms, turning back toward the house and the small entourage that was running toward them.

Abby wrapped her arms around his neck and after a few seconds of holding herself stiffly, she sighed and leaned her head on his shoulder.

It was so innocent that Robert had to swallow a sudden lump in his throat.

He didn't deserve this woman's trust. But he wanted to, so desperately. He wanted to become a man who could make her happy. Not a monster who scared her away.

James and a plethora of servants skidded to a halt in front of Robert, blocking his path.

"Is she well?" James demanded breathlessly, reaching out his arms toward Abby.

Robert felt a surge of protective love as her arms tightened around his neck, and he moved his body slightly so that she twisted away from James's arms.

"I-I'm fine, J-James," she stammered.

Robert looked down at her and saw her blue eyes gazing up at him. Trusting him. Loving him.

With a brief nod for James, Robert stepped around the other man and moved with determination toward the Hall, servants moving quickly out of his way as he went.

The rain pelted him, but he barely felt it. He carried her all the way back to the house, all the while sending thanks heavenwards that she was alive.

And in his arms.

ABIGAIL BURROWED FURTHER under the many blankets wrapped around her as a hive of activity buzzed around her.

She was exhausted, and her ankle throbbed.

But she was loathe to go to sleep until she'd had the chance to speak to Robert. Or at least see him.

The events of the last few hours had been terrifying and wonderful, devastating and marvellous.

It was as confusing as it was frustrating.

Robert had been so cruel to her. Had, in fact, scared her.

Yet when he'd found her by the river, he'd acted as though she were the most precious thing in the world to him.

He'd kissed her and held her close, then carried her all the way back to the house, refusing to let go until he'd laid her on the chaise in his study, and Bessie had to practically shove him away.

What did it mean? Was he just feeling guilty for shouting at her?

Did he feel sorry for her that she'd made such a spectacle of herself over him?

That unpleasant thought brought a wave of shame.

If she'd managed to make herself an object of pity for him, well that would just be the icing on the cake of a truly terrible day.

As soon as Robert had placed her on the chaise, the gentlemen had left the room while Bessie and two of the chambermaids set about making Abigail comfortable.

They peeled soaking garment after soaking garment from Abby's body, before helping to dry her off with piles of warmed linens.

When Abby felt as though her skin had been rubbed raw, Bessie had helped her into a cotton night rail, before wrapping her in her dressing gown.

Abby had felt like a child, unable to do anything for

herself.

But it was nice, she'd conceded as she'd sat at the fire having her hair brushed through, being looked after.

She was quite sure she was too exhausted to carry out any of these ablutions for herself.

Just as Robert had begun banging on the door, demanding to be allowed back into the room, Bessie had placed the last of many blankets over Abigail.

"The duke is beside himself, miss," she whispered for Abby's ears only. "That means something."

But before Abby could question Bessie about *what* it meant, the maid swept away, taking her helpers with her.

The doctor marched through the door as soon as Bessie had left, followed by a still soaking wet Robert, who refused to leave the room whilst Abigail was being examined and obviously hadn't even taken the time to change from his wet clothes. If he got sick because she'd run away, Abby would have that to feel guilty about, too.

It was unorthodox to say the least, and the doctor was most vocally disapproving. One dark glower from Robert, however, managed to silence the older man on the subject. After a brief and painful examination, the doctor left, and James and the dowager entered.

The place was busier than New York with people coming and going.

Abigail looked up to see James, the dowager, and Robert all peering down at her, their expressions ranging from worried, to kindly, to—Abby swallowed at the silver intensity in Robert's eyes—to whatever emotion was blazing in their grey depths.

James, at least, had taken the time to change into fresh, dry clothes.

"How are you feeling, my dear?" The dowager sat gracefully at the edge of the sofa and took one of Abby's hands in her own. "You seem to be warming up."

"I am." Abby smiled. In truth, she felt as though the cold had seeped into her bones, but at least her body was no longer trembling alarmingly.

"I am quite well," she lied.

Her ankle was throbbing and every time she thought of Robert, let alone looked at him, she felt ridiculously tearful.

"You have had quite an ordeal." The dowager gazed at her with eyes so like her son's. "When Robert said you'd fallen at the river—"

The duchess broke off suddenly and darted her eyes to her son.

Abbey followed the woman's gaze and gasped aloud at the look of pain in Robert's expression.

She wanted to jump up and comfort him but of course, she couldn't. Not least because her ankle would prevent her from doing anything close to jumping for some weeks.

And, not to mention, the small matter of not accosting him in front of his mother.

"You are well, and that's all that matters." The dowager patted her hand. "I'm going to go and fix you some warm milk. I used to make it for Robert when he—was younger. It will help you sleep."

Abigail felt as though the dowager was going to say something else but stopped herself.

A lot of that went on around here.

The dowager swept from the room, and James came forward just as the clock struck the hour.

Abigail felt terribly guilty looking into the worried face of her cousin.

In fact, she felt guilty about lots of things.

"I'm sorry to have worried you." She spoke before James could. "And I'm sorry for causing such an uproar in your household." Her eyes flitted to Robert's before skittering away. She couldn't look at him until she could sort out her feelings.

So, probably never, then.

"And-and for ruining your carpets," she finished miserably.

She watched James and Robert exchange a baffled look.

Heaving a sigh, she struggled to sit up a little better under the mountain of blankets.

"I was soaking wet," she explained in exasperation.

"As were you two. You still are!" She glared accusingly at Robert. "And you might get sick because of it. A-and we came in here and dripped all over the dowager's Aubusson carpets, and I feel—I feel terrible about it."

To Abby's horror, she began to cry.

She wasn't overly fond of the carpets. Certainly not enough to cry about them.

"They were beautiful carpets," she bawled.

Abby was embarrassing herself, but she couldn't stop. She didn't care about the carpets! But everything just seemed so *much* at the moment.

She was tired, and cold, and in pain, and in love, which was worse than being in pain. And it was simply too much.

"Abby, they're only carpets," James said placatingly.

But that made her cry harder.

"I don't care about the carpets," she sobbed.

The gentlemen shared another alarmed look, this one tinged with horror, and it would have been funny if she weren't so desperately sad.

Abby bent her head and in lieu of a handkerchief, she used the edge of a blanket to dab at her eyes.

"Go and get your mother," James whispered fiercely.

"No, I'm not leaving her. You go," Robert whispered, equally fiercely.

"I'm not leaving her with you," James bit out.

"And I'm not leaving," Robert repeated stubbornly.

Abby looked up to see them scowling at each other, and she hated that they were at odds because of her.

Another thing to feel guilty about.

And that made her cry harder.

Just then, the dowager swept back into the room, followed by a maid carrying a silver tray.

The older lady took one look at a sobbing Abby along with the terrified faces of James and Robert and shook her head.

She asked for the tray to be left by the side of Abby's chaise, then dismissed the maid with a smile.

"Gentlemen, why don't you give Miss Langton and me a moment or two," she suggested, though her tone left no doubt that this was a demand, not a request.

James's face lit with relief, and he practically ran from the room.

Robert, however, stood his ground, crossing his arms and facing his mother.

The dowager sighed and walked over to place a hand on her son's arm. She leaned in and spoke to him so softly that Abigail couldn't hear a word of what was said.

When she was done, Robert's gaze snapped back to Abby's, and her heart thumped painfully at the intensity in their depths once more.

"I'll be right outside if you need me," he said softly.

If she needed him? Of course she needed him. She

had told him that she loved him, but he'd roared at her to get out.

The pain that lanced through her at the memory made Abigail drop her eyes, whilst shame and hurt washed over her.

How many times would she make a fool of herself over this man?

He didn't care.

Yet his actions suggested that he *did* care.

It was all terribly unsettling.

She heard him leave but didn't look up until the door clicked behind him.

The dowager handed Abby a cup filled with warm milk. The aroma of cinnamon was immediately comforting.

"Let's have a talk, you and I," the dowager smiled.

"What would you like to talk about?" Abby asked.

"Well—" The duchess smiled as Abby sipped her drink. "How about the fact that you're in love with my son?"

Chapter Twenty-Two

ABIGAIL'S HANDS SHOOK violently, and the dowager reached out and calmly plucked the cup from them.

What on earth am I going to say to that? Abby wondered.

Her cheeks flamed with humiliation.

She'd clearly made it painfully obvious to everyone how she felt about the brooding duke.

And now that he'd rejected her, everyone would know of her shame.

To make matters worse, because of her stupid ankle, she was stuck here at Montvale Hall for at least a couple of weeks, meaning she would be ruining the Season for the dowager. The first Season the lady was to participate in for years.

Once again, Abigail's eyes filled.

"I'm sorry," she blurted.

The dowager laughed gently.

"Whatever for, my dear?" she asked.

"For running away. For causing all of this." Abby sniffed. "And for ruining the Season for you. You must wish I'd never come here. I've been nothing but trouble."

"Oh, my dear girl, nothing could be further from the truth."

The dowager sat in one of the armchairs placed either side of the chaise lounge Abby was currently lying on, and leaned forward slightly.

"You being here has given me my life back. It's given me a purpose."

Abigail was touched by the duchess's words. She'd come to love this woman as though she were a mother.

"And whether we go to London now or three weeks from now, I'm happy to just have you in my life."

"I feel the same way." Abigail gave the older woman a watery smile.

"You have been trouble, of course," the dowager continued conversationally. "Heaps of it."

But her grin seemed to indicate that she was rather pleased by the idea.

"And it's exactly what he needs."

Ah.

Robert.

Abigail had managed not to think of him for about seven seconds.

She could feign innocence, but what would be the point?

"He doesn't—" she began. "He can't, or won't, love me, your grace," she mumbled miserably.

The dowager studied Abigail for a moment or two.

"Did James tell you what happened to Robert's sister?"

I killed my little sister.

"N-no." Abigail felt unaccountably nervous. "He said that it was Robert's story to tell, not his."

The duchess smiled.

"James has always been a fiercely loyal friend. As have Simon and Nicholas. And he's right, of course. It *is* Robert's story."

Abigail felt a pang of disappointment.

But the dowager spoke again with quiet determination.

"But it is mine, too," she said softly. "It is about my daughter. And my son. And I want to share it with you."

"NOT EVEN A drink? I think that's a first."

Robert looked up at the sound of James's voice from the doorway.

"It's one in the morning," he said softly. "Gina's anniversary."

James sighed as he came further into the room.

"I know," he said gently. "Are you going to get some sleep?"

"In a while," Robert answered mutinously.

"She's asleep, Robert. Your mother said the laudanum would have her sleeping for hours."

Robert ignored him.

"You know, you're making me feel like a dreadful guardian, sitting in here keeping watch whilst I go about my business."

"You are a dreadful guardian," Robert countered with a grin. "What are you doing leaving a man alone in a room with her?"

James scoffed.

"I can do a great many things, Rob. But moving you away from her isn't one of them. God Himself couldn't do it. A mere mortal has no chance."

It was true. There was no way he was leaving.

His mother had retired around midnight.

She'd come from the study, eyes red-rimmed, and Robert's heart had stopped dead in his chest.

But before he'd been able to launch fully into a panic, his mother had assured him that Abigail was fine and was sleeping. That she'd drunk the laudanum the doctor had given and wouldn't wake again until morning.

He'd been equal parts relieved and disappointed.

He knew that Abigail needed rest after what she'd been through. He knew that her ankle would be hurting and that it was a good thing if she could sleep.

And yet he couldn't help but wish he'd gotten a chance to speak to her. He'd wanted so badly to apologise, to explain.

"I don't like the idea of her sleeping downstairs alone," Robert said, watching the firelight dance across Abigail's face.

"Even with footmen stationed outside the door and her maid in the room?"

"Even then."

James was quiet for a moment more.

"Are you going to tell her about Gina?" he finally asked.

Robert's heart pounded.

"I'm quite sure my mother already did."

"Yes, but are you going to tell her about *you* and Gina?"

He could pretend that he didn't know what James was talking about, but what would be the point? The time for secrets and mysteries was long gone.

Robert had thought he was going to lose Abigail tonight. And that fear had made him realise how important she was.

He could cling to his guilt and grief over what had happened to Gina forever.

Or he could let it go. Try to forgive himself. Try to be whole again, for Abigail.

"I am," he said simply, a world of importance in two little words.

"Are you going to tell her you love her?"

Abigail's words from earlier echoed round Robert's

mind.

Robert, I love you.

She'd been so brave. So honest in sharing her feelings.

And he'd thrown it back in her face.

Could he dare to hope that she'd somehow forgive that? Was he sure that he wanted her forgiveness? He'd been alone for so very long, it was hard to envision a life shared with another.

And Abigail would accept nothing less than all of him. He knew that because he knew her. And she loved with her whole heart. She deserved to be loved that same way.

"I never thought I'd love anyone, James. I'm not even sure I know how."

His friend stood from the chair he'd taken opposite Robert.

Walking over to Robert's chair, he clapped a hand on the duke's shoulder.

"I think your behaviour tonight means you're on the right path," he said ruefully, before walking from the room and closing the door gently behind him.

Chapter Twenty-Three

ABIGAIL AWOKE WITH a start and for a moment, she didn't know where she was.

As her vision cleared, however, the events of the previous evening came rushing back to her.

Her head was pounding, and her mind felt fuzzy.

She remembered the doctor had prescribed her some laudanum to help her sleep through the pain in her ankle.

As though thinking of it had woken the blasted thing, her ankle began to throb.

All in all, she had felt better.

The fire in the hearth was still crackling, to Abigail's surprise, and rather than freezing as she had been earlier, she was uncomfortably warm under the mountain of blankets.

Someone had been tending the fire all night.

She struggled to sit up, her head spinning as she did so.

This was why she hated laudanum. It didn't agree with her at all.

And this one must have been extra strong, for she

had been having the strangest dreams.

She'd even dreamt that Robert and James had been in here with her, whispering, Robert talking of—of loving her.

Clearly the stuff made her fit for Bedlam.

"Abby?"

Abigail yelped at the sound of her name being called.

She managed to sit up in time to see Robert leap from an armchair and rush to her side.

Kneeling beside the chaise, he pushed the blankets back enough for Abigail to breathe properly.

"What's the matter?" he asked, studying her face intently.

"I—what—" Abigail's sleepy mind struggled to put a sentence together. "What are you doing here?" she finally managed.

To her surprise, Robert, the indomitable Duke of Montvale, looked self-conscious.

And she found it incredibly endearing, even after everything that had happened in this very room between them the night before.

Which just went to show what a hopeless case she was.

"You fell asleep after talking with my mother," he said gently.

Abigail's maid hadn't bothered to tie up her hair after it had been dried, and it tumbled around her shoulders now, a lock falling across her brow.

Robert reached out and tucked the strand behind her ear, running his thumb along her cheek before he dropped his hand again.

It was a small gesture, but enough to set her burning up in flames.

"We didn't want to move you with your ankle being injured. So we decided to let you sleep here."

She waited for him to continue, but he stayed quiet, studying her with an unreadable expression on his far-too-handsome face.

But Abigail wasn't about to let him away without answering her questions. Not after everything that had happened.

"But why are *you* here?" she repeated.

Robert grinned wryly, swiftly. But it was so beautiful it was enough to steal her breath.

All too soon, however, it was replaced by his usual stoic mask.

"I—I wanted to make sure you were all right," he said gruffly. "I couldn't stand the thought of you waking alone. Maybe wanting—"

He cut himself off abruptly, and she was left wondering what he'd been about to say.

But then, that was no different to every conversation of theirs thus far.

When the ormolu clock on the mantle chimed, Abby realised it was four o'clock in the morning.

No wonder everything was so silent, so still.

She looked around the room and saw with a start that she and the duke were quite alone.

Her eyes snapped back to the molten steel of Robert's.

"Where are the servants?" she asked, her voice barely above a whisper.

"They're gone to bed," he answered evenly, after a pause.

They were in here alone? In the middle of the night?

"Oh," was all she managed. "You tended the fire?" she suddenly blurted, for want of something to say.

"I did," he answered gravely, but she saw a twinkle of humour in his eye.

She couldn't understand the man. She could spend her whole life trying, and he'd still be an enigma to her.

"How are you feeling?" he asked.

Confused. Nervous. In love.

"My ankle hurts, a little," she confessed. "And my head."

Immediately his brow creased with concern, and he jumped to his feet.

"What can I do? What do you need? Shall I call your maid?"

Abigail laughed in spite of herself.

He looked like a fussing mama.

And try as she might, she couldn't seem to stem the

love she felt for him when he was like this.

When he acted like he cared.

"I'm fine, Robert," she said softly. "Perhaps a drink of water?"

"Water. Right. Yes. I can do that."

Abigail watched in confusion as he moved nervously around the room.

She took in his attire—his rumpled evening jacket, his once snowy-white cravat now muddy and dull that had been loosened, his hair mussed and messy as though he'd been pulling at it for hours. The lawn shirt that was spattered with muck and still damp.

"Robert," she called as he poured water from a jug by his desk. "Have you slept?"

He walked back with a wine glass filled with water and held it out to her.

Their fingers touched as she took the cup, and a shiver of desire ran through her.

Robert noticed and dropped to his knees beside her once more.

"You're getting cold again," he said quietly and fixed the blankets around her once more, ignoring her question.

But she wasn't cold. With him this close, she was burning up.

Had he stayed awake all night? Just sitting there with her while she slept? He must have.

And even though they had discussed nothing. Even

though the last time they'd been alone, he'd broken her heart and scared the wits out of her, Abigail couldn't help herself from loving him desperately.

She held the empty glass out to him, and he took it and placed it on the floor beside the chaise.

He looked back at her, his eyes raking over her as though making sure she was still in one piece.

"You must be exhausted," he said. "You should sleep."

"But we haven't talked," she argued, even though she could feel her eyelids drooping.

The laudanum was certainly doing its job, pulling her back under when she so desperately wanted to stay awake.

"You were so angry with me," she whispered.

Her thoughts were becoming blurrier and blurrier.

She didn't want to apologise for telling him she loved him.

But maybe she'd been too pushy, too—

"Abby." His voice sounded pained. "I have so much I want to say to you. So much that I'm finally ready to say. But you've been through a lot, and you're hurt and tired. Sleep now, we'll talk tomorrow."

Her body was agreeing with him, even if her mind wanted to argue.

She lay back down against the pillow, struggling to keep her eyes open.

"Abby," he whispered.

"Hmm?" she asked, unable to fight the exhaustion any longer.

"I'm so sorry, sweetheart," he said.

She wanted to answer him, but she was so very tired.

The last thing she remembered was the press of his lips against her brow.

Chapter Twenty-Four

"GOOD MORNING, MY dear. How did you sleep?"

Abigail blinked as the harsh sunlight shone through the drapes that a maid was currently opening.

She looked at the ormolu clock on the mantle and saw that it was now ten o'clock.

She usually didn't slept this late.

But then nothing about the past couple of days had been usual.

But after she'd lain back down last night, and Robert had taken his chair, her sleep had been fitful at best.

Though she'd been unable to keep her eyes open, and was both physically and emotionally drained, she'd tossed and turned, unsettling dreams racing through her mind all night, so it felt as though she hadn't gotten any rest at all.

And after a time, sleep had evaded her altogether so she'd lain there, not moving but very much awake.

She'd been so painfully aware that he was in the room.

She could hear his steady breathing. If she concentrated enough, she could catch his sandalwood scent that drove her mad. And whilst she wasn't brave enough to let him know she was awake, she wanted quite desperately to ask him to come and lie down beside her.

So, not only was she an idiot for loving a man incapable of loving her back, she was also a wanton hussy to boot, apparently.

And during those awake hours, Abigail had to make some very tough decisions.

At some point, she must have fallen back asleep, not waking until now.

A memory of last night's conversation with Robert popped into her mind, and she was suddenly fully alert.

I'm so sorry, sweetheart. She hadn't imagined that. Had she?

She sat up, pushing as many blankets as possible off of her, and darted her gaze around.

But Robert was nowhere to be seen.

Abigail supposed it was for the best. It wouldn't do for them to be alone in the study together. Her sleeping in there was already terribly unorthodox.

"Um, very well, your grace. Thank you," she managed to remember to answer the older lady.

"I am having a bath brought to your rooms. When you are ready, we will send for James or Robert to help us get you upstairs."

The dowager chattered away, oblivious to Abigail's

turmoil. For she was remembering how it had felt to be carried by Robert last night.

To be taken care of by him.

He'd kissed her last night when he'd found her by the river.

And right before she'd fallen asleep, hadn't he called her sweetheart?

"Abigail?"

"Yes!"

Abigail snapped her thoughts back to the present.

"I asked if you were ready to bathe, dear," the dowager said serenely.

"Yes. Thank you. I—yes."

"Could you find his grace or Lord Avondale and ask them to assist us, please?" The dowager sent a servant to find one of the gentlemen.

It was only when the room had quieted down and the dowager came to sit by Abigail while she drank the chocolate Bessie had brought in, that Abby got a chance to really look at the older woman.

Her mouth was drawn. Her eyes red-rimmed. And she was as pale as Abby was sure she herself was, from lack of sleep amongst other things.

And suddenly, Abby remembered.

Today was the anniversary of Lady Gina's death.

"Your grace." She reached out and clasped the dowager's hand. "How are you?"

The duchess managed a brittle smile.

"It's—difficult, my dear. But we must go on."

The woman's strength was admirable.

Today must be incredibly difficult, yet here she was, helping Abby.

It was humbling.

The door opened, and Abby's heart leapt to her chest, but it was James and not Robert who stepped inside.

"And how is the invalid?" he asked jovially.

Abigail managed a small smile in response.

James stepped forward and bent to kiss the dowager on the cheek. He gripped her hand for a moment before releasing it.

"Is he well?" the dowager asked softly.

James glanced at Abigail momentarily then turned a reassuring smile on the dowager.

"I haven't seen him," he said regretfully.

So, he'd left. Abby's heart twisted. Would she never learn?

"Right, cousin, let's get you upstairs and fit to be seen." James bent and scooped Abigail into his arms.

She was being terribly selfish, she knew, by wishing that it was Robert's arms she was in, and not James's.

But, she reasoned, if she didn't say it out loud, it didn't count.

And that was the type of flighty thought she hadn't had in so long, that it actually made her feel better.

"It's good to see you smiling, Abby," James said as

he deposited her onto the bed of her bedchamber. "You're not too disappointed about postponing the trip to Town?"

"Since it's my fault, I hardly think I'm in a position to be upset," she quipped dryly. "But no, I'm not disappointed. I think London has lost its appeal," she finished softly, hesitantly.

James had gone to a considerable effort to get her here. Against his will, too.

And now she was being ungrateful.

"You should want to go to London, Abby," he chided. "You should want to meet a man who is kind and uncomplicated. Even manages a smile once in a while."

Abby laughed softly.

But then she sobered.

"You are worried about Robert and me," she said quietly so the servants filling the bathtub wouldn't hear. "But you needn't be. I—I love him, James."

She waited for her cousin to rail against her, threaten to drag her back to New York.

But he merely offered her a sad smile.

Abby took a steadying breath.

Best to get it over with. She'd done a lot of thinking these past few days, and she knew what she wanted.

"He doesn't love me back."

James opened his mouth to speak, but she shook her head.

"He doesn't. And that's—that's fine. But—"

How to explain? How to tell him the conclusion she'd come to in the wee, small hours of the night while the man she loved was so close, yet so unattainably far from her.

"But I know that going to London and meeting a pleasant gentleman who smiles is just not something I can do."

"Abigail, you—"

"And so," she spoke over him, needing to get this out. "And so, as much as I am grateful to you and to her grace, and I really am, I just cannot go to Town to seek a husband. A man I know I won't be able to love."

James looked as though he wanted to say something, but he clenched his jaw and said nothing.

"I want so much to marry for love, James," she said, willing him to understand. "So, if you still want to go to London, I do, too. I want to see it. I just—"

Abby took a deep breath for courage.

"I want to go home when the Season ends. I want to go back to New York."

"You were so looking forward to finding yourself an English lord to love, Abby," James said ruefully.

"And I found one."

Abby's eyes watered, but she furiously pushed her tears away.

"Unrequited love, Abby? You deserve so much more. That can't be enough for you."

Abigail shrugged with a nonchalance she was far from feeling.

"I guess it will have to be."

"You look so much better, dear."

Abigail looked up from her book as the dowager entered the library some time later.

After Abigail had bathed and dressed, she'd been carried to the library.

It was really most inconvenient, being unable to walk.

The doctor had said she would be allowed to hobble around with a stick after a spell but for now, she must keep off her blasted foot.

So, she'd been deposited here with Bessie for company, along with books and trays of food and tea.

And she was utterly miserable.

But she pasted a smile onto her face, regardless.

It wasn't the dowager's fault that her son had mangled Abby's heart.

It wasn't even Robert's fault.

Lord knew, he'd done nothing to make Abigail fall in love with him.

"Thank you, your grace."

"How are you feeling?" the dowager asked, sitting beside Abby and taking her hand.

Miserable.

"Very well, thank you. My ankle hurts a little but tis bearable. How are *you* feeling, your grace?" she asked gently.

"Oh, I'm—managing," the dowager said. "I just wish I knew where Robert was. I worry so."

Nobody seemed to know where the duke had disappeared to.

James had informed Abigail that Robert usually locked himself away in his study with too much brandy.

But he wasn't there.

In fact, he didn't seem to be anywhere in the house.

Abigail looked out the window at the cool, bright day.

The storm that had raged so powerfully the night before had died out, leaving a bright, if weak, sunshine in its wake.

What she wouldn't give to be out in the fresh air picking her wildflowers.

A wave of nostalgia swept over her.

How Robert despised them. Yet he had allowed her to fill his house with the blooms.

"Perhaps he went for a ride," she said, trying to sound reassuring when her own heart was hammering with worry.

Robert had been so miserable last night. In such an awful state.

And though he'd seemed much more in control than after he'd found her by the river, he was holding on to so much pain.

And today would be harder on him than anyone else...

The door suddenly sprang open, and Abby swung her gaze around in time to see Robert walk in.

Chapter Twenty-Five

H E LOOKED...DIFFERENT.

But Abigail couldn't say why, exactly.

He was handsome as ever; his jaw strong, his superfine perfectly fitted to show off the strong, broad shoulders beneath.

His eyes, she suddenly realised, studying him as he came closer.

They were lighter than she'd ever seen them.

They no longer swirled with tormented emotions.

Her heart was hammering painfully, and she could feel her cheeks heat, hoping desperately that the duchess wouldn't notice.

"Robert, darling," the dowager exclaimed, rising elegantly to her feet. "I've been so worried. Where have you been?"

"Apologies for worrying you, Mother." He spoke to the dowager but kept his gaze fixed on Abby.

It was as unsettling as it was wonderful, and her blood seemed to tingle with heat.

"If you'll excuse us, I'd like Abigail to join me outside."

Abby's already thumping heart took flight at the tender look in his gaze.

Oh, Lord. How could she do anything other than love him when he looked at her like that?

"I can't walk," she blurted.

"I know." He smiled that breath-taking smile, and she knew she wouldn't be able to walk when he looked like that, even if she had two working ankles.

Without awaiting another response, he bent down and lifted her into his arms as though she weighed no more than a feather.

His face was so close. Close enough for her to lean up and kiss him.

Which she couldn't.

Could she?

No, of course not!

Robert raised a brow as though he knew where her improper thoughts were leading her, and her cheeks flamed in response.

"Mother." Robert nodded to the dowager, who was watching with her jaw opened, before he turned and marched purposefully from the room.

They passed a delighted looking Bessie on their way into the foyer and a smiling James by the door.

Still, Robert didn't stop, barely sparing a glance for the grinning marquess.

Didn't he realise what a stir he was causing?

Once outside, Abby noticed a shiny, lacquered gig

standing in wait.

Without hesitation, Robert walked toward it and placed Abigail gently onto the bench as though she were made of the finest of porcelain.

He placed a heavy blanket on her lap and a small cushion under her injured foot.

Abigail had to bite back a whimper of longing as his strong fingers grazed her ankle.

And when Robert looked up from his ministrations, his eyes were burning molten silver, with such raw desire that it took her breath away.

She was convinced he was going to kiss her senseless, just like she so desperately craved.

But he stepped back, and the spell was broken.

All the while he rounded the gig, took his seat beside her, and gripped the reins of his matching greys, Robert spoke not a word.

It was only when they'd set off at a slow trot that he turned his gaze to her once more.

"How are you?" he asked.

"Confused," she answered swiftly, earning a soft chuckle.

"I owe you an explanation," he acknowledged.

"Hmm. Or ten," she quipped.

A tense silence stretched, and Abigail could no longer hold her tongue.

"You disappeared this morning," she said, watching his face for a reaction.

He gave none.

But he did answer her.

"I didn't think you'd want my mother and half the household walking in on us sleeping in the same room," he said wryly. "Though technically, I didn't sleep, I would imagine the uproar would be the same."

"You must be exhausted," she said guiltily.

"No," he countered softly. "I feel more awake now than I have in years."

Abigail frowned at the cryptic remark, but he continued before she could question him.

"I had the opportunity to think a lot last night," he said. "Something I haven't allowed myself to do—well, ever. And I've come to some conclusions."

He stopped talking, and Abby wanted to wring his neck and tell him to spit it out.

"Such as?" she prompted impatiently.

"You know, I'm never going to forgive myself for last night." He said it so quietly that Abigail had to strain to hear him.

"Hurting you. Shouting at you. It makes me sick every time I think of it." He laughed briefly, but there was no humour in the sound. "And I can't stop bloody thinking about it."

"It's—"

"Don't tell me it's fine, Abigail. I beg you."

She clamped her mouth shut.

Suddenly, Robert brought the gig to a halt, and

Abigail realised with a start that he'd driven them to the river.

The water was still high and rapid from the storm the night before, and Abigail shuddered inwardly when she remembered how close she'd been to falling in.

But…

This was the river that Robert's sister had drowned in. This was the place he would never, ever come. The place that her actions had forced him to come to last night.

Yet, he was here today voluntarily.

Robert jumped lightly from the carriage and walked around to Abby's side.

Reaching up, he plucked her easily from her seat and slowly lowered her to the ground.

When she was resting on her good foot, leaning against him for support, she looked up at him to see him gazing at her more tenderly than ever before.

Her heart melted, and her knees weakened.

There was definitely something different about him now. And her heart couldn't help but surge with hope.

"I'm sorry, Abby," he said gravely. "More sorry than I can ever say, for so many things."

Abby felt her eyes fill with tears.

"For causing you to have been injured. For causing you to run into a bloody storm."

His mouth twisted in remembered pain.

"I can't begin to explain the fear I felt last night

when I realised you weren't in the house. I died a hundred times over before I found you."

"I'm the one that chose to run into a storm," she reminded him, hating that he was carrying such a burden. Loving that he cared so much.

"Because of my actions," he countered swiftly. "Because I'm the monster who sent you running."

"It doesn't matter," she insisted.

Robert lifted a hand to her face, rubbing his thumb along her cheek.

"You are so courageous, sweetheart. So forgiving."

Abby's mouth dried, and she licked her lips, thrilling at the darkening of his eyes as they concentrated on the action.

"So beautiful," he groaned.

He bent and captured her lips in a soft, gentle kiss.

Abigail sighed, and the second she did, Robert plunged his tongue inside her mouth.

And just like that, the kiss changed.

It was as though a match had been lit and they went up in flames.

Robert pulled Abigail closer still until her body was pressed against the hardness of his own.

Right before Abigail lost all sense of reason, however, Robert pulled his mouth from hers, dragging a hand through his hair.

"God, what you do to me," he groaned. "That's not what I want."

Abigail blinked as a wave of hurt doused the flame of desire.

It must have shown in her face, too, for Robert muffled an oath and took hold of her shoulders.

"I'm making a mess of this," he said. "Of course, it's what I want. I've wanted little else since the day I met you."

Abigail felt a thrill of excitement at his words. He was wreaking havoc on her emotions—from despair to desire and back again.

"But I don't deserve you, Abby. Not the way I am. Not being the monster I've become."

"Robert—"

"No," he interrupted gently. "Please, let me finish. I have so much I want to say."

Abby nodded her consent. Much as she wanted to throw herself back into his arms, she knew how difficult it must be for Robert to be here. And if he wanted to talk, to finally let her in, then she wasn't going to stop him.

Without warning, Robert lifted Abby from her feet and walked a short distance to a nearby tree, placing her gently down to lean against it.

"Wait here," he instructed as he removed his hands from her.

He reached into the gig and pulled out a picnic basket that Abby hadn't noticed.

She stood watching in amazement as he made his

way to the riverbank and proceeded to lay out blanket on top of blanket.

Finally, he came back to her and once again scooped her into his arms.

Abby immediately wrapped her arms around his neck, sighing happily, and smiled up at him.

"If you keep looking at me like that, I'll get nothing said," he warned gruffly, and Abby's stomach flipped.

Shaking his head slightly, as if to clear it, Robert carried her the short distance to the blankets, where he set her down before taking a seat beside her.

"The ground is still wet," he explained. "I hope there are enough blankets to keep you dry."

"It's fine," she said, touched that he was being so considerate.

"I hardly know where to start," he began with a wry smile. "It's a first for me, talking in any real way to anyone."

He glanced over at her, and she noticed that his eyes were once again the colour of storm clouds.

"But then, I've never had anyone I wanted to open up for," he said softly, and Abigail had to give herself a stern talking to so she wouldn't throw herself at him.

"I need to start by apologising. Not just for last night but for so much of my behaviour from the time you arrived here. Truth be told, we didn't often get visitors, and that was my fault. After—" He took a deep breath, and Abigail's heart ached for him. This was obviously very difficult for him.

"After Gina's death, I locked myself away as much as I could. As soon as I finished school, first Eton and then Oxford, I came straight home and hid away as much as possible."

He was quiet for a moment, but Abigail didn't try to fill the silence, as was her wont.

He needed to get this out, and she desperately needed to understand him more.

"You heard about Gina's death?" he asked, turning back to her briefly before moving his gaze once more to the river.

"I did," she whispered. "Some of it—your mother told me she—that she drowned?"

Robert stiffened visibly, and Abigail reached out and grasped his hand, unable to help herself in the face of his despair.

Instead of pushing her away, Robert turned his palm so he could lace his fingers with her own.

He studied their entwined hands as he spoke.

"Gina was the most impulsive child I'd ever known, apart from my friends and I," he smiled swiftly.

"The day she died—there'd been a storm the night before, not unlike last night, and the river was danger-ous. She insisted on coming after my friends and I as we set out exploring." He paused. "I should have sent her back."

Abigail wanted to tell him that it wasn't his fault.

That nothing he'd done had caused his sister to die.

But she remained quiet.

"She climbed that tree," he nodded toward the willow that Abby herself had sat at last night, before slipping. "I told her to come down but—"

He swallowed hard.

"The branch snapped. She fell in. And I—I froze. Only for a moment, but it was long enough for her to go under."

Abby's tears fell freely. For the poor little girl, for the man beside her who never should have had to witness something like that.

"I went in after her. I even managed to hold onto her. But she slipped away. I couldn't—I couldn't get her back. I tried. But my friends pulled me out. I *let* them pull me out. And then—she was gone."

Abigail dashed her tears away impatiently. She tightened her grip on Robert's larger hand, wishing his pain away.

"If I'd sent her back. If I hadn't hesitated. If I hadn't been so selfish as to let them pull me from the water, Gina would be here now."

"Oh, Robert."

But he wasn't finished. It was as though a dam inside him had burst, and the words were pouring from him.

"She'd probably be married. My mother might have even been a grandmother."

He heaved a sigh and shook his head sadly.

"She died because of me. And my father took the news so badly that he drank himself into an early grave only seven years later."

Suddenly, he jumped up from beside her and began to pace back and forth, the words tumbling from his mouth.

"After my father died and I became the duke, the guilt became too much. *Living* became too much. I couldn't stand to see people happily living their lives around me. I couldn't stand the ghost that my mother had become, knowing that she'd become that because I had been responsible for taking away her daughter and her husband."

No! How could he be carrying such awful, misplaced guilt around with him? It tore Abby's heart out.

"So, I locked myself away. Got the reputation of a monster—cruel, gruff, uncaring, and unfeeling. And I relished it. After all, nobody would ever try to get close to a monster."

He stopped pacing and swung to face her, a riot of emotions stamped across his face. Then, his face cleared and his eyes grew tender.

"Until you."

Chapter Twenty-Six

ROBERT FELT WRUNG out. Exhausted from speaking aloud the words that had consumed him for so long.

He looked down at the woman who had captured the heart he no longer thought he possessed, and that same organ twisted as he realised she'd been crying.

He never wanted to make her cry. Not ever again.

But he needed her to know. To know all of him.

All last night, all this morning, Robert had faced his past in a way he'd never done before.

He'd faced it, and he was learning to put his demons to rest. For her.

Because Abigail deserved so much more than the man he'd been. She deserved someone whole. Someone free to be happy and just love her as someone as wonderful as she warranted.

Robert didn't think that was him yet. But he loved her far too much not to try.

She deserved the truth.

She had told him that she loved him, but his demons, the monster inside him, made it impossible for him to accept the gift of her love and return it with every part of him.

Which is what she deserved.

But there were parts of him that belonged to the past he couldn't outrun. The past he couldn't forget.

And the only way he could be the man she deserved was to forgive himself for his past mistakes, and try to let them go.

Abigail began to struggle to stand up, and Robert immediately dropped to his knees beside her.

He didn't want her trying to stand on that ankle.

His gut twisted with familiar guilt. He'd done this to her.

He really was a monster.

"Don't try to get up, love," he said softly, and he watched her eyes widen at the endearment.

How could she not know that she was his love? His everything.

But then, he'd never told her.

Well, he'd started telling her everything, and he would finish. He had to. For both their sakes.

"I've never spoken to a soul about this. I never felt the need to. I honestly thought I'd live the rest of my life isolated and alone. I *would* have, if it wasn't for you."

Robert reached out and wiped a tear from her satiny soft cheek.

Even now, even when he felt wrung dry emotionally, the desire for her flared hot and fierce.

"All night while you slept, and all this morning, I've faced up to my past in a way I never have before. I've faced up to my feelings in a way I wouldn't have. Because I didn't do it for my own sake, I did it for yours."

He reached out and grabbed her tiny, delicate hands, gazing into the impossibly blue pools of her eyes.

"Last night, the second you left, I regretted my actions more than I can say. And when I saw you slip on that riverbank, the same one that destroyed my childhood, I thought my life had ended in that moment. That was when I knew for sure, I don't want any sort of life without you in it."

Abigail gasped at his words, but Robert didn't allow himself to be distracted.

"Nobody else would have gotten me to this riverbank," he said wryly. "That's why I brought you here today. To show you that I'm no longer running from my past. No longer allowing it to control me and make me a monster."

He gazed at the woman across from him, wondering if she had any idea how beautiful she looked with the sun dancing off her golden curls and the tears swimming in her eyes making them bluer than he'd ever seen them.

"I don't want to be a monster anymore. Because

you deserve more than that. I don't want to hide myself away. Not from you. You deserve a man who can love you freely, without being weighed down by sins of the past."

His heart was thumping, and Robert felt like a nervous schoolboy.

Taking a deep breath, he smiled one of the few real smiles he'd ever managed.

"And I want to be that man for you, sweetheart. Because I love you."

Robert didn't know what he'd expected Abigail's reaction to be.

More tears, maybe.

Even saying she loved him, again.

What he certainly hadn't expected was for her to launch herself at him, throwing her arms around him, and planting a kiss on his mouth.

Robert felt a moment's surprise before his body reacted to the feel of her in his arms and within seconds, he'd taken control of the kiss, wrapping his arms around her and lowering her to the blanket below them.

He pulled his lips from hers, his eyes drinking in the image of her, plaint beneath him, her tremulous smile melting the remnants of the ice around his heart.

"Do you really, truly forgive yourself?" she surprised him by asking.

Robert thought about her question, had thought

about nothing else for hours.

In the early morning, before dawn, he'd allowed himself to imagine if he and Abby had children.

He'd faced the painful idea of a tragedy such as this befalling them.

And Robert knew, he would never blame a son of his, a mere child, for a tragic accident such as what had happened to Gina. And he had realised then, that's what it was—a tragic, terrible accident.

Robert had allowed himself to acknowledge that his fourteen-year-old self couldn't have done anything differently.

Then he'd imagined abandoning Abigail and any other children they had, turning his back on them and spending his days drinking himself to oblivion, slowly killing himself day by day, drink by drink.

And no, he had realised, he wouldn't do that either.

He would make a different choice to the one his father had made. And that's what it had been. A choice. His mother had said as much, and Robert believed her now.

He would always mourn the loss of his sister, and even his father.

He would always miss the old duke and grieve for the life Gina should have known.

But he would no longer blame himself for things outside his control.

"I do," he answered, smiling down at the woman

who had single-handedly given him his life back. "I forgive myself, and I am ready to let go of the past."

Her smile was dazzling.

"I love you," she said simply, and his heart burst.

"Even for shouting at you and sending you out into a storm?" he asked.

"Even for laughing whilst the storm ruined my dress," she answered tartly, earning another of those laughs.

He leaned down and touched his forehead to hers.

"Thank you for bringing me back to life," he whispered.

"Thank you for letting go of the monster," she whispered back.

Robert grinned and smoothed a hand down her body, eliciting a moan that drove him half-crazy.

"I find there are far more pleasurable things for me to hold on to." He grinned wickedly before bending to press a trail of kisses along her jaw.

Abigail reached up and clasped his face in her hands, dragging his mouth over to meet her own.

And there by the river, Robert said goodbye to his demons, and hello to his future.

"ARE YOU SURE it's all gone?" Abigail demanded as she once more reached up to pat at her head, searching for grass.

She had visions of entering the Hall and the dowager immediately knowing what she'd been getting up to with the older lady's son.

Robert laughed and the sound was so light, so carefree, that her heart almost burst from hearing it.

It was hard to believe that only yesterday, Abigail had thought she would lose him forever. Had believed him too lost to his past to ever have a future with her.

And now—she sighed happily—now he would be hers forever.

"I'm positive. Do you really think I'd take you in there with any hint of what we've been up to? I've only just decided to look forward to the rest of my life, my love. I don't want James ending it with a shotgun."

His love.

Nothing had ever sounded more wonderful.

"Well, we'd best get inside then. Your mother must be beside herself. We've been gone so long."

"Not long enough," Robert grumbled as he jumped down and walked around to her side of the gig.

He lifted her from the conveyance, planting a kiss on her lips as he swept an arm under her knees.

"Much as I want your pain to ease, I think I'm going to miss having to carry you everywhere," he whispered in her ear, and Abigail couldn't hide the shiver of desire that coursed through her.

His wicked grin was proof that he knew exactly

what he was doing to her.

"There's always the other ankle," she said a little breathlessly. "Even a couple of knees."

Robert laughed as he carried her up the steps and into the foyer of Montvale Hall.

Abigail couldn't stem her gasp as her eyes took in the sight before her.

Everywhere she looked there was vase after vase of wildflowers.

They adorned every available surface, bursts of colour and scent.

"Robert," she turned her gaze back to his. "What is all this?"

He winked as he carried her toward the drawing room.

"This is the result of hours of back-breaking flower picking," he said seriously.

They reached the drawing room, and Abigail's eyes widened at yet more vases filled to bursting with flowers.

James and the dowager were standing in the centre of the room, matching grins on their faces.

"I can't believe you did this," Abigail whispered to the man holding her, her eyes filling yet again. She was surprised she had any tears left.

"Of course, I did this," he answered simply.

He lowered his face toward hers, and Abigail felt an expectant thrill shoot through her.

"Ahem."

The sound of the duchess delicately clearing her throat brought Abigail's mind back out of the gutter and to the drawing room, where Robert's mother and Abigail's cousin were watching them.

Her cheeks heated immediately, but a quick glance showed that their smiles were well and truly in place.

Robert looked marvellously unperturbed.

He walked the short distance to a blush coloured chaise, and placed Abby on the cushions.

He hunkered down in front of her, taking her hand and ignoring the other occupants of the room.

"Do you like it?" he asked.

"I love it," she immediately responded. "But why did you do this? I know you hate them," she finished mischievously.

"Minx." Robert grinned. "I told you they've grown on me. I couldn't be without them now."

His thumb stroked a lazy circle against her palm, sending all sorts of tinglings along her nerve-endings.

The double meaning of his words weren't lost on her, and audience or no, she reached a hand up to smooth against his jaw.

"You have brought so much beauty and colour to this formerly desolate place," Robert said softly. "I thought you deserved to see beauty and colour for yourself."

Oh, how she loved him. Who would have thought

this man before her was the monster whom she'd met when she'd first arrived?

Robert leaned closer, speaking so that only Abby could hear.

"I've been thinking. Perhaps we should leave that ankle and those knees intact," he said.

"Oh? And why is that?" she asked, leaning closer, too.

"Because I want you to be able to walk down the aisle to me as soon as possible," he answered.

Well, how could she not kiss him senseless after that?

The dowager and James would just have to avert their eyes.

Nothing else mattered to Abigail at that moment. Nothing but the monster who had learned to love.

THE END.

Epilogue

"**N**OT GETTING COLD feet are you?"

Robert looked up as James entered his study, followed by Nicholas and Simon.

For the past couple of days, guests had been arriving, filling Montvale Hall with more people than had ever been seen.

Robert would have had a small, intimate wedding. Had even tried to insist on it. Old habits did die hard, after all.

But Abigail had insisted on a wedding fit for a duke. And everyone already knew that Robert couldn't deny his future duchess anything.

"It's not for me, Robert," Abby had said, *gazing up at him with eyes that should be weaponised. They rendered a man useless. A slave to her. "But your mother would be so happy. It's the least we can do."*

"I hate the idea of a large wedding," he'd sulked.

He'd denied sulking, of course. But sulk he had.

"I do, too," she had grimaced. *"But I don't care how I marry you, as long as I get to be your wife."*

So, here they were, three long months later, on the morning of the wedding of the year.

The banns had been read while they'd been in London.

The dowager had insisted that Robert stay at James's Grosvenor Square townhouse, a stone's throw from his own.

And she'd kept Abigail so busy that Robert had hardly gotten to spend any time alone with her.

He'd even had to brave those blasted Society events, just to get the chance to hold her.

It had been worth the sycophantic fawning, the scandalised whispers, even other men's lascivious stares at his fiancée, just to get to hold her. Just to get to breathe the same air as her.

"It's no use, James," Simon's voice sounded from the drinks table, dripping with disdain. "The man can't string a coherent sentence together anymore. Not unless it's about the delectable Abby."

That got Robert's attention, and he scowled at Simon, even as the other man handed him a tumbler of brandy.

"Watch your mouth," he growled, and the other three gentlemen laughed.

"It's not my fault you're marrying the most beautiful woman in England, Robbie," Simon laughed, and Robert gritted his teeth.

He hated that name. And Simon knew it.

"Simon, ease up on him," Nicholas, ever the peace-keeper, called from the fireplace. "He's nervous," he finished with a grin.

"Remind me again why I invited you all." Robert knocked back the contents of his tumbler, choosing to ignore the raucous laughter of his oldest friends.

"I'm giving Abigail away," James reminded him. "So there's no getting rid of me."

"And I'm here to try to convince you to come to your senses," Simon drawled, his looks and countenance a study in opposites to the blonde and jovial James. "Marriage," he finished with a shudder.

"Don't knock it," Nicholas said seriously. "You never know, you might find yourself caught in the parson's trap one day."

"Over my dead body," Simon responded sharply. "I would have put money on you or Golden Boy over there being the only ones to wed."

James made a crude gesture in response to another of Simon's despised nicknames.

"But lo, someone has managed to take down the Monster of Montvale Hall."

Robert raised a brow at his friend.

"All the more reason why the Devil of Dashford should be in trouble," he mocked, earning another shudder from Simon.

"Bite your tongue," the other man commanded laughingly. "It will take more than a blonde beauty to

THE MONSTER OF MONTVALE HALL

tame the Devil," he finished with a wink.

Robert didn't bother arguing.

Abby was so much more than a "blonde beauty."

She had saved him.

And in just a few short hours, he'd have her all to himself.

"Um, Robert, I'm terribly fond of you, but the look on your face right now is making me deuced uncomfortable," Simon said. "I'm afraid you're not my type. Far too hairy."

"Oh, God," James spoke up. "Don't look at him. He's been nauseating for months now. I can always tell when he's thinking of Abby because he looks like that." James pointed a finger at Robert. "And since she's my cousin, and more like a little sister, it doesn't bare thinking about."

Robert glanced at Nicholas, usually the voice of reason, and his only hope for sense and sanity amongst their group.

"Care to chime in?" he asked.

"Sorry." Nicholas grinned. "I am, of course, happy for you, but even I'm finding it hard to stomach the moon eyes."

"Laugh all you want," Robert told the others as he stood and began to put his jacket on.

If there was a slight tremble in his fingers, his friends didn't need to know about it.

"I will remember to mock you all mercilessly when

it happens to you."

James walked over and clapped Robert on the shoulder.

"All joking aside," he said seriously, "I couldn't be happier for you, Rob. For you and Abby."

Simon rolled his eyes.

"Saint James strikes again," he said as he led the way out of the study and into the carriage waiting to take the men to the estate church.

"Says the Lord of the Sinners," James bit back.

Robert let their bickering wash over him. In a few short minutes, he'd be with Abby again. And nothing could dampen his happiness at the thought.

"THE DUCHESS CERTAINLY knows how to throw a party," Abigail whispered some hours later.

"You are the duchess now, sweetheart," Robert reminded her by whispering in her ear and causing her blood to sing.

The wedding ceremony had been perfect.

When the church doors had opened to admit her and James, Abigail had been a bundle of nerves.

But then her eyes had caught Robert's, and the look on his face had chased away everything but the thought that she was about to become his wife.

Now they were waltzing and even though the ballroom was full to the brim, Abby felt like they were the only two people in the world.

"Have I told you how beautiful you are?" Robert asked, his eyes molten silver.

Abby shivered in response.

"Hundreds of times," she croaked. "But I'm not complaining."

The white lace gown had been commissioned by a mantua maker in London when they'd gone there for the end of the Season. The weeks of fittings, and prodding, and poking had been worth it the second Robert's eyes had darkened as they'd raked over her.

That look had heated her skin so much, Abigail had been surprised when her bouquet of wildflowers didn't go up in flames.

"I can't wait to get you all to myself," Robert growled, pulling her scandalously close.

"Careful, husband," she whispered impishly. "Your monster is showing," she finished with a wink that earned her a bark of laughter and more than one shocked gaze.

Everyone, it seemed, was finding it hard to reconcile this laughing, happy man with the one they'd known before.

"Only for you, sweetheart," he smiled wickedly.

Abby almost swooned from desire, and she was dangerously close to ruining her reputation by accosting her husband there and then in front of all of their guests.

She was saved from herself, however, by the arrival of James at their sides, his face pale, his blue eyes grave.

"James, what's wrong?" she cried, alarmed by the seriousness in her cousin's face.

James was always so jovial, it was a shock to see him looking so bleak.

"Apologies for the interruption," he said, and something in his voice caused Abigail to grab onto his arm.

"What is it?" she asked.

Robert put an arm around her shoulder, and she was grateful for his strength.

"It's Thomas," James bit out tersely.

Thomas was James's younger brother.

Abigail had never met him but by all accounts he was a rouge, flitting from continent to continent without the pressures of the marquessate to worry about.

James sighed and ran a hand down his face.

"He's dead," he finally blurted.

"Oh my goodness, James," Abby cried, unsure what to say.

Robert silently reached out and grabbed his friend's shoulder.

"I just received word," James said quietly, ensuring that nobody around them heard their hurried conversation. "A letter from Vienna."

"Who wrote you?" Robert asked.

"I don't know. It wasn't signed. It said that Thomas had been killed, and I should expect the arrival of an important artefact to Avondale."

Abigail frowned.

"And it wasn't signed? None of this makes sense," she said.

"I know," James agreed. "But I must return to Avondale immediately. If only to find out what's going on."

"Let us help," Robert said, but James shook his head.

"It's taken you far too long to get here, my friend," he said with a genuine smile. "I can handle whatever this is. I'll send word as soon as I know what the hell is going on."

Without another word, James turned on his heel and fled the ballroom.

Abigail looked up at her husband.

And even in the seriousness of the situation, she felt a thrill of pleasure at calling him that.

"Do you think he will be all right?" she asked.

Robert smoothed an errant curl from her brow.

"I think he'll be just fine, love," he smiled. "He knows I'm here if he needs me. But he also knows I have very important things to deal with here."

"Indeed?" she asked as Robert began to expertly steer her toward the opened doors of the ballroom.

"Such as what?"

"Such as escaping the festivities with my wife," he answered with a grin that made her toes curl. "Such as stealing a few moments alone so I can kiss you how I want, feel you how I crave, and tell you properly how madly in love with you I am."

By the time they were in the hallway, Abby was nearly expiring with need.

With a darting look around to ensure they weren't being watched, she grabbed her husband's hand and ducked into a small morning room, locking the door behind them with a decisive click.

And then twined her arms around her husband's neck and proceeded to kiss him how she wanted, feel him how she craved, and show him, without words, how madly in love with him she was.

THE END.

Thank you for reading *The Monster of Montvale Hall*! I hope you enjoyed Robert and Abigail's journey to happily ever after. If you enjoyed this story please leave a quick review on your favorite book retailer. Reviews help other readers determine to try my books or not, and I love reading what you thought! If you want to learn about my new releases, or when my books go on sale, please follow me on BookBub, or subscribe to my newsletter.

Keep reading for a special preview of *The Angel of Avondale Abbey.*

The Angel of Avondale Abbey

BY
NADINE MILLARD

Prologue

"FATHER, PLEASE BE reasonable. If you continue down this path, Thomas might never come home."

James knew that trying to reason with his father was likely a lost cause. But he would try nonetheless. Because his mother would have wanted him to. Because his grandmother had asked him to. And James always did what was asked of him.

"Your brother is a spoilt, selfish scoundrel, James. And he needs to be taught a lesson."

The Marquess of Avondale was unyielding. His youngest son was out of line and if he didn't get back into it, he'd be cut off. It was as simple as that.

James often tried desperately to get his father and Thomas to understand each other, to make the marquess see that to Thomas, his father couldn't care less about him.

James was the heir. That made Thomas the spare and he felt it keenly. And Thomas acted out accordingly, always desperate to get their stern sire's attention.

Thus far, the only attention he had managed to

garner was negative. But something was better than nothing, Thomas had told James.

They looked alike, he and Thomas. But looks were where the similarities ended.

Since boyhood, James had taken his role as heir seriously. And he'd done so with good humour and grace.

He was always pleasant and kind. Always willing to help when he could, wherever he could.

His friends at Eton had called him the Golden Boy.

It helped the moniker stick, he supposed, that he had a mop of bright golden hair.

Thomas was a study in opposites.

Irresponsible, dissolute, debauched. He spent his life flitting from gaming hells, to mistresses, and back again.

Tales of his scandals regularly made the Society pages, earning his father's constant disapproval, and his grandmother's shame.

It didn't help matters that when they wrote about Thomas and his evil ways, they inevitably compared him to James, painting the latter as a paragon of all that was good and right in the world.

This tended to upset Thomas even more, causing him to act out in wilder and wilder ways.

And James was always expected to clean up his messes.

Which is how he came to be in his father's study

this morning, a study that would one day be his, begging clemency for his younger brother.

"Let me talk to him," James said now. "Give him a chance to—to grow up. He's still young."

"As are you, James, yet you do not bring shame upon our family name every time you leave the house."

No, James thought bitterly. He never acted out. He was always good. Always well behaved. Always...staid and dependable.

Boring.

"Just give him one more chance," James begged.

His father studied him for a moment or two, before sighing and leaning back in his leather desk chair.

"Fine," he conceded. "One more chance. If Thomas can keep his bib clean for the rest of the Season, I'll continue to pay his allowance. If not, he's cut off."

"Thank you, Father," James said jumping up before his father could change his mind. "I'm sure he'll appreciate your generosity."

He slipped from his father's study, into the corridor beyond—and straight into his brother.

"Pleading my case to dear old Papa, were you?" Thomas slurred and James realised his brother was in his cups. Again.

"A little early for whiskey, is it not brother?" he asked, trying to move Thomas away from the door of the study, lest his father realise what state he was in.

"Not if you haven't been to bed yet," Thomas

drawled.

The brothers entered a small sitting room and Thomas pulled his arm from James's steadying hand.

"Thomas, I've spoken to Father and—"

"And saved the day, just like always."

The sneering in Thomas's tone, the hatred in his expression, took James by surprise.

He'd always fought Thomas's corner, always defended him as best he could.

James felt a spurt of anger at Thomas's attitude.

He'd spent the morning arguing against the marquess cutting Thomas off without so much as a guinea to his name, and this was how he'd repay him? With derision and sarcasm?

Just once, James would have liked to be the son who didn't walk the straight and narrow.

His friend Simon, the Earl of Dashford, was perpetually encouraging James to be a rogue, just once.

Alas, with Thomas having painted himself firmly as the black sheep, that left only responsibility and familial duty for James.

"Don't blame me for your poor decisions," James bit out, his patience fraying. "Clean up your act or you'll be penniless by month's end. I managed to buy you some time, but Father's tolerance won't last forever."

His younger brother studied him closely, and James began to feel slightly uncomfortable with the scrutiny.

"Let me guess," Thomas finally spat, his eyes the same shade of deep blue as James's glinting with icy fire. "Father offered to give me some time as a favour to *you*, the Prodigal Son."

James resisted the urge to pull at his cravat.

For Thomas spoke the truth. Father wasn't doing this for Thomas. He was doing it because James had asked it of him.

"I never asked for the disparity in our treatment," he whispered. He wouldn't insult Thomas's intelligence by pretending it didn't exist.

Time and again he'd spoken to the marquess about it but to no avail.

Thomas's lips twisted in a sardonic impression of a smile, but James saw the hurt flash in his eyes.

"You're a good big brother, James," he said now and the derision was gone from his tone. Replaced by something akin to desolation. "But even you can't make the old man love me."

"He loves you," James argued at once, even though he wasn't entirely sure that it was true. "He just—"

"He just doesn't need or particularly want me," Thomas finished.

The brothers faced each other, a world of differences in the feet separating them.

"You know," Thomas said after an age, "I don't think England is for me any more. I think it's about time I found pastures new."

"You're taking a Grand Tour?" James asked.

It mightn't be a bad idea, at that. Thomas wasn't long out of Oxford and plenty of young gentlemen made the trip before settling down to whatever role had been pre-ordained for them.

James and his friends weren't back long from theirs. Only Robert, the Duke of Montvale, had refused to join them. Robert's father had only recently passed when the friends had decided to travel, and besides, Robert would never dream of doing anything that resembled fun.

But he, Simon, and their friend Nicholas the future Duke of Barnbury had all spent months travelling around the Continent and were all the more well-rounded for it.

It could be just the thing for Thomas. Something to make him mature and settle. Get all the wildness out of his system.

"I think that's a good idea, Thomas. You'll benefit enormously from it, I'm sure. And once you're back, you can decide what you want to do with your life."

Thomas smiled at his older brother, but there was an odd sadness to the expression.

"Thank you, James," he said. "Sincerely. I am well aware that I've always had my big brother watching over me."

He left quietly, and James felt unsettled at the odd

sense of finality about his brother's words.

Little did he know that when Thomas left the room that day, he'd left for good.

Learn more about
The Angel of Avondale Abbey by going here.
nadinemillard.com/saints-and-sinners

About Nadine Millard

Nadine Millard is a bestselling writer hailing from Dublin, Ireland.

When she's not writing historical romance, she's managing her chaotic household of three children, a husband and a very spoiled dog!

She's a big fan of coffee and wine with a good book and will often be found at her laptop at 2am when a book idea strikes.

Connect with Nadine!
Website: nadinemillard.com
Newsletter: eepurl.com/dNCiX-
BookBub: bookbub.com/authors/nadine-millard
Amazon: amazon.com/Nadine-Millard/e/B00JA9OXFK
Facebook: facebook.com/nadinemillardauthor

43877988R00182